FOR MY PARENTS

NOTE

The headings at the beginning of each chapter are written in either Old Norse (medieval Scandinavian) or Old English. Both languages were in use during the ninth century, and there was a certain amount of mutual intelligibility.

CHAPTER ONE

❧

grand-viðar
bane of wood (literal translation)

FIRE

❧

Now that it's over, the whole thing has the quality of a dream when you wake up in the morning, where the more you try to remember it, the more hopeless it gets, like trying to hold onto water in your cupped, leaking hands. And I mean all of it, not just the weird stuff. I mean Cressida and Tim, and their cold, dim house full of beautiful objects from all the interesting places they'd been to when they were younger; I mean Mr Richards, with his heather hair and his Welsh lilt. Those things are fading as fast and getting as misty as the rest of it. The weird stuff that can't possibly have happened really – except it did, and I've got the scars to prove it.

The village was called Hoxne. You say 'Hox-un' if you're a local and in the know, which I definitely wasn't. And Sofia, driving me there in her buzzy little social worker's car – 'paid for by my taxes', Tracy said, with a sort of false, automatic bitterness, learnt from other people, which was a bit of a joke actually, because when had Tracy ever earned enough to pay even one penny in tax? Anyway, Sofia called it Hocks-nee too, because she was from Romania or Spain or somewhere, and was as much of an outsider as I was, when you came to think about it.

I was going there because Tracy burnt down our house. She really did burn it down. She fell asleep with a lighted cigarette in her hand after drinking about fifteen vodkas, and the cigarette set fire to the sofa. There were fire engines and gawping neighbours, and a five-minute piece on the local television news. It was the first time she'd done anything as bad as that, but she'd been on their radar anyway and it was the final straw. 'The final straw in the coffin', Sofia had said, displaying a grasp of English idiom that was not quite faultless. She'd given me a stupid cartoon leaflet explaining what it meant, being 'in care', and now we were zipping along the A140 towards a village neither of us knew how to pronounce, and further and further away from Ipswich and Tracy and the twins, who were staying in town and being fostered together in a big house by the park.

'I think you will like Cressida and Tim, Joss,' Sofia said.

I said nothing. Which I believe is often the best thing.

'They are very musical – Tim plays the piano. And

Cressida gives violin lessons. And they keep chickens. I expect,' Sofia added vaguely, 'that they grow organic vegetables.'

The last of the light was draining out of the sky, and I no longer recognised any of the names of the villages on the road signs. On either side of the road, the trees and hedges were lumpy and black against the milky violet of the evening sky.

I felt a breathless kind of panic, as if someone was trying to stuff me into a sack.

My world was buses and shops, the solid reassurance of pavements under your feet, and the cold, clean light of kebab shops spilling out of plate glass in the middle of the night. The air I was used to smelled of petrol, and not like this air, of emptiness. I knew that Hoxne – Hox-un – was buried deep in the guts of the Suffolk countryside, and I was trying very hard not to let the thought of it frighten me, but it did. It scared me, the emptiness. Breathe. Breathe.

'Be a good boy, Joss,' Tracy had said. Her hands were shaking when she fished in her bag for a tissue. There was a deep groove between the long, vertical bones in her arm. Tracy never had the time to eat.

'I'll see you once a week. At a family centre in Diss. And Sofia's enrolled you in a new school. It'll be better than that dump you're in now.'

A fierce, tearing not-quite-pity had shot right through me.

'Oh, well, you're sixteen,' Tracy had said.

She started to pick at the flaky skin around her nails.

'When I was sixteen, I had you on the way. It's time you grew up a bit.'

In the back of the paid-for-by-taxes car, I wondered out loud how much bloody further it could be.

Sofia flashed me a tense, false, teeth-gritted smile in the rear-view mirror.

'Almost there, Joss.'

The house was right on the edge of the village, up a tiny lane only just wide enough for one car, and it was bigger than any house I'd seen before. Bigger than any house needed to be. Sofia pulled up outside the front door, and we got out; she opened the boot, and I took out both my bags, which suddenly looked small and familiar and shabby and sad. I blinked and looked away.

It was one of those drives that curves all the way around, one way in and another way out, made of shingle like on a beach. My shoes made a crunching sound whenever I took a step. And the house was even bigger, once you got up close. It was bigger than the whole block at Ipswich had been. The faded purple paint was flaking from the windows and doors; I could hear the soft bickering sound of the organic chickens, but I couldn't see them. They must have been round the back.

'And here is Cressida.'

She doesn't look real, I thought.

I didn't know why the words banged into my head, and then I realised: it was her clothes. They weren't the usual sort people wore; they were long and sort of drapey. More like dust sheets covering a statue than clothes. And there was a big hole in the elbow of the jumper she was wearing. Her hair was strange too, pulled into a wispy grey tail over one shoulder.

She looked like someone in fancy dress.

'Tim's in the kitchen,' Cressida said. She squeezed my arm, which normally I would hate, but for some reason it didn't bother me at all.

'This way. We'll have a cup of tea, and it won't seem so strange. Tea's the same wherever you are.'

'We've had a long talk, Joss and I,' Sofia said, 'about *acceptable behaviours.*'

Cressida didn't answer, only smiled. When she moved her head, the last of the daylight caught what looked like diamonds hanging from her ears and made them flash.

'Through here. This is Tim, Joss.'

I squashed down a laugh at the sight of his beard, which was so wide and bushy that a family of small animals could have nested in it. He wore little glasses, round as coins, which were pushed up onto the top of his head, where they nestled in the tufty hair. When he smiled, I saw he had a gap in between his two front teeth, which somehow made me want to trust him.

You could fit the whole of the ground floor of our home into the kitchen at Cressida's house. There was room for a sofa, which was something I'd never imagined you would have in a kitchen, and a big, square cooker thing which pumped out so much warmth I could feel the sweat forming in the roots of my hair.

'That's an Aga,' Cressida said, seeing me look at it. 'It

roasts us alive in the summer, but in the winter we have to climb inside it to keep warm. The rest of the house is Arctic, I'm afraid. It's so old, it's falling apart.'

Tim shook my hand.

'I'm a bit garlicky. I'm sorry,' he said. 'Been cooking all afternoon.'

He was wearing an apron, I noticed. I had never before seen anyone wearing an apron. And the kitchen looked like a bomb had hit it, only it was a different kind of mess to mess I'd seen before. There were bits of fruit and vegetables and stuff lying around on chopping boards, lumps of meat and blocks of cheese. Packets of flour and bottles of oil. Stuff like that.

'Tim's not what you call a tidy cook,' Cressida said. 'Now, shall we get comfortable? And Sofia can have a cup of tea before she goes back.'

My legs felt suddenly watery and I sat down quickly on the sofa.

Cressida sat herself down next to me.

'You'll be all right, Joss,' she said.

People say it all the time: 'You'll be all right.' And usually it means nothing. Or nothing much anyway. Just that they like you and want you to know it. But the funny thing about Cressida saying it, was that it sounded truer than that. Like she knew more than I did. Like things really would turn out OK in the end.

Suddenly, I realised something. I realised that I liked Cressida and Tim. And that you could trust them.

11

～～

And then, the next bit: the first day at the school Sofia had enrolled me in, the one that Tracy said was better than the Ipswich dump I'd gone to before. Which wouldn't have been difficult. I wasn't expecting Eton or Harrow or wherever it is rich people send their kids; I wasn't expecting anything, which I believe is often the easiest thing to do. I didn't want to be, but I was nervous.

Cressida offered to walk with me to the village green where the bus stop was, but I said don't bother. I think I had some stupid, hopeful idea about fitting in.

Fitting in, hah!

I couldn't have been more conspicuous if I'd painted my face blue and arrived at the bus stop on a unicycle. I felt their stares jabbing me even though I kept my back turned and my eyes fixed and gazing over the village green, as if I could see something fascinating happening in the far corner of it.

I'd heard of village greens before, but this was the first time I'd actually seen one. The kids were nothing new though – different faces, different uniform, but apart from that, nothing I'd not seen a million times before. It was as easy as it always is to see who was who. The hard ones were standing around smoking and the quieter, more timid ones were clutching their instrument cases. The girls were grouped in shrieking huddles, laughing and tossing their hair about. I'd seen it all before.

And then I noticed her – a girl with fair hair standing

quite still and apart from the rest.

Her aloneness was why I noticed her. Because I think you don't often see girls on their own – they usually flock together like birds. Noisy birds, making a great show of their happiness. But this girl stood apart from the others on the pavement between the grass and the bus stop, and there was nothing in the easy lines of her body to suggest she felt awkward in the solitude. And you felt like all she had to do was crook her little finger and friends would come running. Like she was only on her own because at the moment she wanted it that way. She was calm and self-possessed, which was the impression I was trying to give as well, only my arms and shoulders were starting to ache from the effort.

She was too far away for me to make out the colour of her eyes.

The sun was already hot, and the shadows of the trees were sharp and black on the grass. A village green. It sounded like something you read about in books, but here it was in front of me: a broad expanse of short grass, roughly rectangular in shape and dotted with trees. Round the edge of the grass were houses, some painted shades of white and others made of warm-looking orange bricks. Pretty much all of them had those windows that are criss-crossed with strips of wood or metal, so they looked like illustrations in a children's book, not quite real. Some of the roofs were thatched. I was glad when the bus came.

Easterbrook School was about twenty minutes away by bus, down more of those narrow lanes I'd come along in

Sofia's car. No one spoke to me, which was all right because I had nothing to say to any of them. And I noticed, in the curious, detached way you notice that it's raining outside, that no one on the bus had my skin colour or my hair. Like, literally no one. Suddenly, despite the stab of recognition a few minutes earlier, these kids seemed like creatures from a different world.

There were two of them waiting for me when I stepped out of the bus at Easterbrook, a girl and a teacher, both of them wearing bright, eager Welcoming expressions.

'I expect you're Joseph. I'm Ms Osborne, headteacher. Welcome to Easterbrook.'

She was a pale, skinny woman, wearing a mouse-coloured jacket much too big for her. She reminded me of something; then I realised what: a lizard. There was something reptilian about her face, despite that Welcoming smile.

'Yes. I'm Joss.'

'We're very pleased to have you, Joss.'

Both of us knew that this was a lie. I started to enjoy watching her going through the motions. It wasn't her fault, any of this, but then neither was it mine, and it was fun to watch her squirm.

'And this is Rachel. She's going to show you around until you get settled in. I've put you in Mr Richards' class.'

Her shoulders twitched inside the roomy jacket; she was clearly longing to be away.

'Do you have any questions?'

None that you could answer. I shook my head and was

rewarded by a brief flash of reptilian smile.

'Fine. Stick with Rachel. Come and see me if you have any problems or issues.'

I didn't know, and I bet she wouldn't have known either, what she meant by *issues*. I turned to look at Rachel, who turned out to be exactly the kind of frizzy, motherly creature who would be asked to go round with the new boy and keep an eye on him.

'Come on, then. We'll go to class. Mr Richards is a bit weird, but he's nice; you'll like him. He's head of history. I'm going to take history for A level, next year. Have you decided which A levels you'll be doing?'

It was like the harmless twittering of birds. I looked past her, over the frizzy head, to what I thought for a second was the fair-haired girl from the Hoxne bus stop coming through a set of double doors to the right, only the face was wrong, and it wasn't her.

' ...History, English Language and dance. I'm staying on for sixth form because it's the best one in the area. It's nice to have GCSEs over with, isn't it? Only results day to worry about.'

'I'm not worried,' I said.

It wasn't an empty boast; it was true. I couldn't have cared less about results day and A levels. I could barely remember sitting the exams, and it had been less than three weeks ago. Tracy had been clever too, at least as clever, I would bet, as bespectacled, twittery little Rachel, and look where it had got her. Nowhere, that was where.

She blinked and giggled and carried on twittering.

'Here's the classroom. Up those stairs over there it's the Year 11 common room. It's nothing much, just a room with a microwave and lots of chairs.'

☯☯

The fight, if that's what you want to call it, started in the common room during the lunch break.

'Half a day,' Ms Osborne said to me, 'half a day before there was trouble. What kind of impression do you think that gives us of you, Joseph?'

She looked at me sadly, but behind the sadness you could see the satisfaction easily enough.

I said nothing. Although what I wanted to say was that I couldn't care less what kind of *impression* I'd made.

I'd managed to shake off Rachel and was sitting minding my own business when I'd heard noises from a corner of the common room – the raised voices and jeering kind of laughter that tell you someone's in trouble. I glanced up, but I wasn't that interested. I'm not the sort who likes getting involved in other people's business. And I wouldn't have done, only something in the eyes of the kid they were tormenting caught me. He was a skinny, specky kid, the kind that carries a briefcase and is ridiculously good at maths. And he looked like he was about to start crying any minute, which is not something you want to see, even if it's none of your business. Two bigger kids were holding him back and another was indolently going through the contents of his case.

'It's a poem! He's actually written a fucking *poem* about her! I'll read it out, shall I?'

He cleared his throat and held out the scrappy piece of paper he'd taken from the briefcase.

The kid's voice was clogged with tears.

'Give it back, Rufus, don't be like that, please Rufus...'

'*To Alice.*'

Rufus read out the words slowly and loudly. From where I was sitting, across the room, I could feel the kid's eyes filling with tears.

'*Here is my innocence/Lying beside us in the grass/Take it, for it is yours...*'

Gripped on either side by the two bigger boys, the briefcase kid slumped in defeat.

I didn't know why, but I was up and crossing the common room before I had time to think or plan anything. Rufus glanced at me, and then back, histrionically, to the poem. I was walking normally, not looking at them, like I was just going to walk out of the common-room door.

Use the element of surprise, Mr Finch used to say. Mr Finch was the coach of the dump-school football team. He'd had a rigorous tactical system based on positioning and quick, accurate passing; and knowing, at every moment and without looking up, where your teammates were. He'd drilled it into us till we could do it in our sleep. But he also encouraged us to act impulsively: a darting run, a looped kick above the defence; a volley from an improbable angle.

Do the unexpected, Mr Finch used to say, looking like a balding owl behind his black-framed thick glasses – they can't plan for that.

Of course, if you did the unexpected and it didn't work, he'd rave and shout till the spit collected at the sides of his mouth about being too bloody thick to stick to a simple system, so you couldn't really win.

But it worked this time.

On my way to the door I turned and flicked the paper away from Rufus. He gawped comically for a second at his suddenly empty hand, and then his face darkened into anger.

'What the fuck—'

'Stop being a dick, *Rufus*.'

The boy with the briefcase wriggled away from his captors. I handed him his precious poem.

'There you go.'

He didn't dare to look his thanks. He stuffed the poem into his pocket and scuttled out of the door.

I followed him. I heard Rufus say, 'Who do you think you are, anyway?' but the swing of the closing door cut him off.

It wasn't the end. I knew that. Everything about his smooth, good-looking face; the drawling way he spoke; the stupid friendship bracelets that went all the way up from his wrist to the elbow – all of it told you how much he thought of himself. He wouldn't be able to laugh it off, being made to look like an idiot by some newcomer on his first day. I knew his sort and they always had to win. Winning; it's like a disease with some people.

❦

It took him half an hour, that was all. I'd known he was watching me – I could feel his eyes on me even if I didn't turn round to look. So I'd zipped round the school trying to lose him, and into a different toilet to the one by the common room, which would have been like walking into the world's most obvious trap.

I can piss and be gone again in fifteen seconds, but it wasn't quick enough. I was caught in the trap anyway.

There was Rufus and three others. The little kids who'd been there when I came in skittered away like mice, and one of the Rufus-army situated himself by the door, a massive grinning guard.

Rufus wasn't smiling. His smooth face had gone hard and ugly with hate. This wasn't about some silly kid who I'd stopped him bullying, or if it was, it was just the excuse he gave himself. This was because I was different. It wasn't race, because one of the henchmen was blacker than I was. It was because I was from somewhere else, a different part of the jungle, and he hated it. He would stamp on me like you stamp on a cockroach.

Rufus licked his lips. He stiffened his neck, the way people do when they're psyching themselves up for a fight.

He said, 'Get hold of him. I'll find one they haven't flushed, the dirty little sods.'

He poked his head in and out of each of the cubicles.

'This'll do.'

Both my arms were gripped. I head a soft snort of

laughter from the guard at the door.

It was ridiculous. They were going to shove my head down a dirty toilet, and all because I was from a different tribe. It wasn't personal, because they didn't know me from a can of paint. They hated me because I wasn't one of them, and that was all.

I felt myself being dragged closer to the cubicles. I took a deep breath.

CHAPTER TWO

❧

grennir-gunnmass
feeder of ravens (literal translation)

WARRIOR

❧

I fight dirty, even though I'm not a dirty person. It's just that I believe – no, I know – that when you fight fair, you've put yourself at a disadvantage from the word go. If you fight fair, it seems to me, they're going to grind you into the dust. It isn't right, but it's just the way it is.

He was taller than I was. I had to stretch right up to bring the bony bit of my forehead crashing down onto the bridge of his nose. I heard, rather than felt, the eggshell splintering of cartilage; I heard his yelp of pain and felt the warm spatter of blood against my own eyelids.

He staggered backwards, pressing both hands to his face. I could see bright red blood flooding helplessly between his fingers. He fell forwards onto his knees, and the blood began to drip from his face onto the chequered tiles on the floor.

I pulled myself free. It was easy. The hands holding me had gone soft and limp like flounders.

'Maybe remember this next time you think about picking on someone who can't fight back,' I said.

I stepped over Rufus, who'd curled up into a ball still holding his face, and left the toilet.

I didn't see him again that day. I suppose he went home. Mr Richards murmured his way through registration, and there were lessons in the afternoon, but I couldn't have told you what they were about. And then at about three o'clock, I was summoned to Ms Osborne's office so she could let me know how Disappointed she was in me. She managed at the same time to let me know that she wasn't the least bit surprised.

And why would you be? A kid who's in care, a background of chaos and muddle and one crisis after another. A burnt-down house on the worst of the Ipswich estates. Something like this, those hooded reptilian eyes were soundlessly saying, was bound to happen, wasn't it?

'There will have to be consequences, Joss,' she said, 'you know that, don't you?'

I didn't say anything. Of course I knew it. There's something about people like me that attracts trouble the way a dead cat attracts flies. Consequences, hah!

I sat by myself upstairs on the bus, not thinking about any of it, because what was the point of thinking? It was so hot by now that the air felt sort of thick and wet, and there was none of the usual shouting and messing about that goes on normally on school buses. The windows had been cranked open as far as they would go, but no breeze had found its way in. The deep, endless lanes the bus was trundling down were so narrow that the trees and bushes scratched at the glass, filling the top deck with a liquid green light.

She got off the bus just ahead of me. She was wearing headphones, and I wondered what music she was listening to. I would have liked to guess, but it was impossible.

The current of hot, sweaty black-clad schoolchildren broke up into eddies as kids went their different ways: across the green, up the cramped little street with its shops, over the road to the shiny new houses that had been built in a horseshoe shape to try and convince you they'd been there for centuries.

The sweat was tickling my back. I got my phone out and jabbed the screen. I wasn't supposed to text Tracy, but how would they ever know? And I wanted to talk to my friends, the ones I'd left behind in Ipswich. I didn't have anything to say to them particularly, but I wanted to talk to them even if it was only to reassure myself they were still there.

'You won't get a signal.'

Close up, her skin was smooth as cellophane, and faintly flushed with the heat. At some point during the day, she had plaited her hair into two braids, which made it look darker than in the morning, when it had been pouring blonde and straight down her back. And the ends of the braids were the exact same shape and size of the bristles of a child's paintbrush.

'There's no signal at all in the village, it's awful. We're the back end of nowhere here,' she said.

When she smiled, I noticed how white her teeth were. Everything about her looked fresh and brand-new and perfect. I felt sweaty and used-up standing next to her.

'I was going to text home,' I said.

'Oh, yes,' she said, 'you're the new boy, aren't you? The one there was all the fuss about.'

Her voice was thin and silvery. It sounded all the time like she was on the edge of laughing, only not quite.

'You might get a signal up there. Climb through the copse, you should be able to text,' she said.

'What's your name?' I asked.

She smiled, and I knew that she'd been waiting for me to ask.

'Alice. And you're Joss.'

She hitched her schoolbag further up her shoulder.

'Do you want me to show you the way? It's not far. Just over the green and up the hill. Shall I come with you?'

She stepped closer, and I caught the scent of her: a flowery perfume-smell but underneath it, just cleanness

– clean clothes clean skin clean hair. I could wash for a hundred years and never get to be that clean.

'Don't you have to be anywhere?'

She laughed. 'This is Hoxne, Joss. There isn't anywhere to be.'

She set off across the green, and I followed her.

'Alice. Was that poem about you, then?'

'I heard about that,' she said, 'I wasn't there but I heard about it. Apparently you half-killed Rufus in the boys' loos afterwards.'

'Rubbish,' I said, 'and anyway, he started it. If you start something, you should have the balls to finish it. Someone should tell that to Rufus Whatever-his-name-is.'

'Palmier-Thompson. This way. Through the copse and then over the bridge. You're higher then, you see. Sometimes there's a signal.'

'It was you though, wasn't it? In the poem?'

'Oh, I don't know,' Alice said easily. 'I think so. Probably. It's not my fault, but that David…he's always had a bit of a thing about me. And Rufus doesn't like it. He probably wanted to humiliate him, teach him a lesson.'

Humiliate; the word sounded horrible in her mouth, lumpy and smug. I wished she hadn't said it.

'Keep off the grass, you mean. Is Rufus your boyfriend?'

'No. Why?' She looked up at me through her lashes, and I suddenly felt like telling her to stop playing games. It hadn't been a game for whatshisname, David. Or me, come to think of it. I'd probably be sent somewhere else now. And I liked Cressida and Tim, and the big, cool, dark

house and the organic chickens. So stop it, I wanted to say,
stop with the Bambi eyes and acting all arch and innocent.
It's real for me, even if it isn't for you.

'Alice?'

'What?'

'What the hell is a copse?'

It turned out to be a word for the little wood, but it wasn't
a wood really, just a group of slim trees on the edge of the
green. The flickering green and gold shade from the leaves
was cool on your back after the sun.

'God, it's hot,' I said.

'Want some water?'

Alice unzipped her bag and fished out a water bottle.
She was so organised, so perfectly well equipped. Already
I was beginning to know her – efficient and serene and
perfectly certain of her place in the world. She and Rufus
Palmier-Thompson, aimed like a pair of unassailable
arrows at A levels and decent universities and Glittering
Academic Careers. I pictured viola lessons and horse-
riding, holidays in France where she'd speak the language
and eat the food without turning a blonde shining hair.
Nothing seemed too good for her, her suntanned limbs and
perfect, unscuffed sandals. I wasn't sure if I liked her yet,
but there was something fascinating about the perfection.

'Can I ask you something, Joss?'

We were at the edge of the copse; up and to the left was

the bridge she had mentioned. I knew what was coming. I knew Ms Osborne, or someone like her, must have explained to the Easterbrook year group something about the special circumstances that had brought me here, and how patient and understanding they needed to be. I knew it, because it always happened that way. Girls always started off by feeling sorry for me. Especially ones like Alice. It drove me mad, if you want to know the truth, like all I had to offer anyone was a sad back-story. Like they're going to get a big kick out of rescuing me.

'Why I'm here?'

'Yes. Don't tell me if you don't want to.'

I shrugged. 'It's not a secret. And I'm not ashamed of it.'

She waited and drank some more water.

'I'm here because I'm in foster care. With Tim and Cressida, over there somewhere.'

I indicated vaguely down the hill. 'Because of Tracy. My mum...she's a bit useless. They're going to have to decide whether to take us off her permanently. Well, not me, maybe. I'm nearly seventeen, but my sisters are only two. They'll be adopted, no problem. People like babies.'

'They're twins?' Alice said, making her eyes go wide. Girls always liked talking about my sisters. I didn't know why.

'Yeah. Virginia and Sylvia. Tracy likes reading. Well, when she's not off her head she does. She wanted to do literature at UEA, but she had me instead. Downhill all the way after that.'

'What nice names,' Alice said.

'Yeah. They're going to stick out like sore thumbs at school in the middle of all those Avas and Amelias, but I think they're great names.'

I swallowed. I'd told Alice I wasn't ashamed, and I wasn't. But I didn't like thinking, even for a second, about the twins. It made everything harder to bear.

I felt Alice slip her hand through my arm. I still wasn't completely sure I liked her, but my skin prickled at the touch.

'This way. Over the bridge,' she said.

Still with her hand linked through my arm, we stepped onto the wooden boards of the bridge.

'I don't think you need this bridge,' I said. 'You could step over this stream. Maybe it was bigger once, like a proper river.'

'It's a special bridge,' Alice said. 'There's a legend about it. If a couple crosses it on their way to get married, it's bad luck and the marriage will be a disaster.'

'I think we'll risk it,' I said. 'I haven't known you all that long. It's a bit early to start talking about marriage.'

Alice laughed and tucked her hand in tighter.

'It was in Viking times. What do you call them...the Dark Ages? King Edmund was hiding under it, after some battle or other with the Vikings. Then someone told them he was hiding there, and they dragged him out and shot him full of arrows. He became a saint eventually. You know, like in Bury St Edmunds.'

'My auntie Pauline used to live in Bury St Edmunds,' I said.

We were over the bridge now. Now we were no longer in the little wood – the copse – the sunlight was so fierce it made you squint.

'The bridge thing,' I said. 'What's it got to do with bad luck and weddings?'

'Well, because of the legend,' Alice said, 'which says it was a couple on their way to get married that gave him away. They saw his gold armour shining in the water and told the Vikings where he was. They've put you in Mr Richards' class, haven't they? I'm surprised he didn't tell you about it as soon as you walked into the room. He's boringly expert about the Anglo-Saxons. I think he's had a book published about them.'

'I've got better things to do at school than listen to Mr Richards talking,' I said.

I hadn't meant anything in particular by saying that, but she must have thought I meant her because she blushed.

'Try now. You can sometimes get a signal from here,' she said.

The trouble was that now I had signal, I found I didn't know what I wanted to say. I sent a quick text to Tracy and another one to Harry Fraser, who was the closest thing I had to a friend in Ipswich. I'd hung around with a lot of people – Tracy used to complain if there too many of them in the lounge, dropping ash on the carpet and talking so loudly she couldn't hear the television – but Harry Fraser had been the only one I'd actually liked.

'Are you texting a girl?' Alice asked.

I shook my head and put the phone back in my pocket.

'My mum and my mate; that's all.'

We went back, hands not touching any more, back over the bridge and down through the slim trees, towards the green.

After the glare and sticky heat, the inside of Cressida and Tim's house was as cool and dark as a well. My eyes took a moment to adjust. The air was filled with a rich smell of chicken cooking from the kitchen. I dropped my schoolbag on the tiles next to a grandfather clock I hadn't noticed the day before and went into the living room to find Cressida.

She was sitting by the open French doors, reading a book and wearing glasses that magnified her eyes and made her look very peculiar.

'Hi,' I said.

'Joss, hello. I've made some lemonade, look. It's boiling outside. The radio says it's hotter in London than it is in Madrid.'

'Ask me how my day went,' I said.

Cressida took off her glasses and laid them on the table. 'I have a feeling I already know how your day went,' she said.

I said nothing. Of course the school would have phoned. Getting their version in first. It wouldn't be true, it wouldn't even be halfway true, but it would have hardened into truth by the time I got home on the bus.

'Miss Osborne phoned me. She said there'd been a fight

in the boys' toilets, and that you injured someone.'

'*Ms*,' I said furiously. 'You have to call her *Ms* Osborne.'

Cressida poured some lemonade, and then she put out her hand and patted me. Normally, I hated people touching me, but just like before, I didn't mind Cressida's little pat. In fact, it made me feel soft and tender inside, and as if I might cry. But I never cried, not ever.

'Jesus would have turned the other cheek,' Cressida said, 'but I expect you're going to tell me that wasn't an option.'

Her tone was mild and ordinary, like she was talking about the weather or something.

'No, it bloody wasn't an option,' I said.

Her mentioning Jesus had made me feel hot and prickly and uncomfortable. Going to church, singing hymns, all that stuff. Believing. It's one of those things I just didn't want to think about and whenever I did think about it, I could never understand it, how people could believe in something they couldn't see.

'Well,' Cressida said comfortably, 'if you say it wasn't an option, then of course I believe you.'

'I'll be sent back though, I bet,' I said bitterly, 'sent somewhere else, I mean.'

I realised as I was saying it that I didn't want to leave. If I couldn't go home to Ipswich and Tracy and the twins, then I wanted to stay here in Hoxne with Cressida and Tim.

'Tim and I will fight very hard for that not to happen to you,' Cressida said.

'I was provoked,' I said, 'but they won't believe me. I

know they won't.'

'I believe you,' Cressida said again.

The evening passed. Cressida finished giving violin lessons in the downstairs front room they used for music; we ate the chicken thing. Ms Osborne called again, about six, and spoke rapidly and breathlessly into the answering machine: there would be a meeting on Thursday. Until then, I was to stay away from school.

'They love meetings,' I said. It sounded flat and helpless when I said it, because it was. It was hopeless.

'Tell you what. Borrow my bike after supper.' Tim said, 'Go for a bike ride. That always makes me feel better. It's impossible not to feel happy when you're outside on a bike.'

To please him, I said that I would, and to please him again I agreed to borrow some Lycra shorts and a black top covered in writing that stuck to me like a layer of cling film.

'You're more aerodynamic that way,' Tim said, 'and you don't get trouser legs caught in the chain.'

'Tim's a mammal,' Cressida said, smiling so that the skin round her eyes crinkled like cracks on a china plate.

'A middle aged man in Lycra. A MAMIL.'

It was a joke, and so I smiled, but the truth was I felt ridiculous. I drew the line at a helmet. He gave me one, but I took it off and left it in the front porch.

Tim's bike was battered and elderly, a little like Tim himself, but he had strapped a fancy, new-looking satnav to the front handlebars. I was touched, really, that he'd trusted me with it. It must have been worth quite a lot.

Impossible to be unhappy on a bike, he'd said, and for about half an hour, while the light lasted, he was right. My legs ached with pedalling, but it was a good pain. And the air rushing past gave me a fresh, exhilarated sort of feeling. But as it grew darker, I began to feel something else: a squirming, knotty sensation, and after a second I knew what it was: fear. Which is not like me, not at all. I had no idea where I was, but it wasn't that which was making me afraid. In any case, I had the satnav. It was more like that shifting, uneasy feeling you get when you think someone is watching you. I knew there wasn't anybody there, but I still felt like I was being chased. I cycled faster and faster in an effort to outstrip the fear.

But it was no good. I felt like I was being pursued: by Rufus Palmier-Thompson and Ms Osborne; by all the social workers I'd known over the years, all the advisory teachers and counsellors with their calm voices and their Listening expressions. All the meetings, where nothing Tracy could say would ever make a difference. All the useless, oddly similar men drifting in and out of her life like taxis. Craig Kevin Billy David Chris. Tears and shouting. Rows about money owed and letters from the council about housing benefit. I pedalled harder and harder, trying to outrun them all.

☙❧

It was properly dark now. The sky had turned inky black and was speckled with stars. The light at the front of the bike was powerful, but it was small and it only made the darkness feel like it was pressing in on either side. My chest began to feel tight, the grey fist of asthma threatening, just out of reach, to squeeze and crumple my lungs like two paper bags.

And then my front wheel hit something sharply, and I felt myself falling forwards and up. Then down, and down. Cressida had said something about an old quarry, I thought, and then I hit the ground with a hard crunch and a sweet, complete blackness wiped me out like chalk from a board.

CHAPTER THREE

❧

gear dagum
days of past years (literal translation)

PAST TIMES

❧

W hen I opened my eyes, I could see nothing at all apart from a whiteness so bright it was like someone shining a very powerful torch in my eyes. It was so bright, it hurt. It had been night when I fell, and now there was nothing at all apart from this hard, painful light.

Oh God, I wasn't *dead*, was I?

The idea that I might be was so huge and horrible that I couldn't think of anything else. I lay back and waited. Maybe if I kept very still and quiet everything would be normal again.

And then a shape began to form itself in the whiteness. It

was blurry at first, but the outline got sharper and sharper until I could make out a face, with two dark blotches for eyes and another one beneath them for a mouth. The mouth-blotch was moving but all I could hear was a dull booming sound, the way things sound when you're underwater.

I tried to move, but when I did, there was a shooting pain in my shoulder that seemed to spear right through me down to my feet. I closed my eyes again, but the dull, underwater boom continued.

Maybe I was concussed. I'd fallen off Tim's bike and down into the quarry Cressida had warned me about, and I must have banged my head on something on the way down. I would just lie still and wait for the whiteness and the pain and the low booming noise to fade away.

Except they didn't; I opened my eyes again and the hard white light was still there, and the blurry outline of a face with the moving mouth. And then the face sharpened into clarity, like when you adjust the focus on a telescope, and I could see that it was a proper face, a man I had never seen before, and that he was leaning over me. His face seemed to swim in the whiteness, which I saw now was a bright, pale sky. He was looking concerned.

'Are you all right?'

Weirdly, I understood what he said even though the words weren't the right ones. I don't know how else to explain it. It was like he was speaking a foreign language, except I understood every word. I could see more clearly now, and I saw that the man had a dirty face and long hair that was matted almost into dreadlocks.

What was going on?

I tried to speak but could only make a groaning noise.

I could hear the singing of birds, suddenly loud. There was a strong, ripe smell in the air that seemed to scorch the back of my nose and throat – it came, I thought, from the two dead hares the man was carrying on a stick held across his shoulder. Or maybe from the man himself. They were knotted together like scarves – the hares, I mean – and hung head down, bleeding slightly from the mouth.

I shook my head, the way you might shake a radio to re-tune it. It hurt, and I made the groaning noise again.

'Where are you hurt?' the strange man asked again.

Whether I was dreaming, or concussed at the bottom of a quarry, or dead; whichever it was, I was touched by the concern in his eyes. And his hands when he touched me were cool and gentle. His words were the same peculiar mixture of normal English and incomprehensible gabble as before, but in the mad logic of dreams I understood him perfectly. And – and this is the seriously weird bit – when I answered him, my own words were in the same nonsense language, and yet I understood them perfectly as well.

I said, 'My shoulder...' except, like I said, it came out sounding quite different. He knew what he was doing, but I swear I had never felt such pain in my life. He helped me to sit up, felt both my shoulders and made the kind of face people make when they're trying to decide if a picture is level. He put both his hands on my left shoulder and twisted swiftly. There was an audible 'pop'.

'It's gone,' I said, as soon as I could speak. 'I don't know what you did, but the pain's gone. God, what a relief... thank you.'

He laughed. 'It wasn't anything very much. Your bones were out of line, that's all. You must have hit the ground with a terrible smash. What did you do? Trip over a blade of grass?'

'I don't know how it happened,' I said. It was the truest statement I had ever made.

He helped me stand up.

'Can you bear weight?' he asked.

Carefully, I tried first one foot and then the other.

'I think so. It's just my head that hurts a bit.'

'You can lean on me, if you like,' the man said.

He was wearing a dress. A sort of shapeless tunic thing that ended just above his knees. Around his shoulders he was wearing what looked like a grey blanket. His legs were encased in baggy leggings the colour of mud. And...oh God...I was dressed the same.

Obviously, I was dreaming. I was lying at the bottom of the quarry, concussed and dreaming.

'Are you Jesus?' I asked.

I sounded stupid, but I thought he might be, because of what Cressida had been talking to me about earlier. Sometimes stuff like that finds its way into your dreams.

'What? No, I am Penda, son of Ethelred. What is your name?'

'Joss, son of Tracy,' I said, 'where's my bike? I mustn't lose it – it isn't mine to lose.' I thought Tim's bike might have vanished, the way my clothes had disappeared, and even though I knew it was only a dream, I felt anxious and guilty. Tim had trusted me.

Penda, son of Ethelred, looked round vaguely. I saw his face change as he noticed, at the same time as I did, the front wheel of Tim's bike sticking up at an angle from the long grass a couple of metres behind us. I found I had been holding my breath, and I sighed with relief.

Touching it gingerly, as if it was a bomb that might go off at any moment, Penda tried to right it. He set the wheels spinning, grunted in what sounded like recognition, and then tried to stand it up. He was clumsy, and the front wheel was pointing almost backwards.

'Careful! You'll break it,' I said.

I unzipped the saddlebag, and found that my phone and my inhalers were still there. The phone was dead and useless but when I pressed one of the inhalers, a chemical-scented puff emerged, hung on the air for a second and then disappeared. 'What do you call it? What a strange machine! Like a cart…but where do you put things?'

'Here, like this,' I said.

I straightened the wheel and put my hands on the handlebars. Penda was frowning like he was trying to figure out how it worked.

'You don't put things anywhere. It's not a cart. You sit on it, and ride along,' I said.

'Ride? Like on horseback?'

'Yeah, I suppose like on horseback,' I said. I was trying to see if the bike was damaged, but it didn't seem to be. The wheels still went round, which was the main thing. But the satnav thing was totally dead. I flicked it off and on again, but the screen stayed dead and black. I squeezed my eyes tightly shut and concentrated very fiercely to wake myself up. Sometimes you can drag yourself out of a bad dream by force of will. But not this time. I opened my eyes, and it was all still there: Penda, the birds singing their heads off, and me in the sack-shaped dress and mud-coloured leggings.

'Where are you headed for, Joss?' Penda asked.

I couldn't think of anything to say to this at first, and then I remembered Hoxne, with its village green and bus stop and tidy, coloured houses.

'Hoxne,' I said, only it came out quite different.

'Haegelisdun? Oh, well, you're almost there. It's my village – you can come with me. Where have you come from?'

Penda was friendly, but the smell – coming off either him or his dead hares or both – was making my throat clog up. I took quick, shallow sips of air, and tried not to gag.

'I'm from Ipswich,' I said.

He seemed astonished and impressed, like I'd said I'd just arrived from Timbuctoo.

'Gipeswic! You must have had the protection of heaven to travel so far in safety.'

His face creased in what looked like embarrassment.

'But Joss, tell me. The colour of your skin, your hair…is this the way people look in Gipeswic?'

He reached out a dirty forefinger and gently touched my

hair, just above my left eyebrow. I could see fascination in his eyes, mixed with amusement. And pity.

'It's...it's strange hair, Joss. And no mistake.'

This from a man wearing a dress and baggy tights.

'Some people look like me. Not everyone,' I said.

He grinned, showing yellow stumps of teeth.

'I always thought things would be very different in Gipeswic. Come, let's go. And we should sing,' he said.

'Should we?'

'Only outlaws and thieves creep about silently like foxes. Good Anglo-Saxons sing and make clamour. To ward off trouble. And let others know we mean no harm.'

I thought, oh, Anglo-Saxon. It wasn't Jesus and turning the other cheek that had lodged in my brain and sparked this confused and concussed dream, but Alice and Mr Richards and a conversation about Vikings and armour and a bridge. The Anglo-Saxons, about whom Mr Richards was so boringly expert.

'All right. What shall we sing?'

Penda taught me the complicated words and barely discernible tune to a song about a battle, and I taught him the simplest football chant I knew. We alternated singing them for half an hour or so, walking back through a sunlit wilderness of trees and hedges and birds singing, and not a trace of any other people. We took it in turns to push Tim's bike. Penda had completely lost his fear of it, and slung the dead hares casually across the handlebars to save carrying them.

I heard and smelled Haegelisdun before I saw it.

The real Hoxne – the one where Cressida and Tim lived, and where I was presumably lying unconscious on the ground somewhere – was a quiet place, neat and pretty and unmoving as those pastel scenes on tins of biscuits, or a child's jigsaw. But this Haegelisdun, the one we came to abruptly rounding the corner by some young, yellow-green trees, buzzed with noisy life and the sharp stink of lots of animals.

'Home at last,' Penda said.

That first sight of the village hit me with the force of a blow. I stopped walking, and Penda bumped into me from behind. There was so much to see and hear and smell that it was like my brain couldn't keep up.

There was no sign of a village green. Instead there were houses scattered across a broad patch of land, not in rows or circles or groups, but randomly as if dropped there from above. They were wooden, more like biggish garden sheds than proper houses, and the roofs were thatched with bushy straw. It was buzzing with people, all looking more or less like Penda. The noise, once you got properly close, was a roar. A long pole, like a giant lathe, was turning round and round as someone worked wood, and gave off a sparking, shrieking sound. A skinny brown pig barrelled past, banging into my legs and squealing.

I felt breathless, like I'd been punched in the stomach. It had to be a dream, but it wasn't a normal dream. It was a strange, busy, detailed nightmare. Except it looked so real. It *was* real.

Penda shouted something, but I couldn't hear him.

I took a deep breath to try and steady myself.

'What?'

'Aesc isn't here. He's away till sundown, at least. I'll take you to Wuffa.'

I shouted back, 'Who?' but he was pulling me past a pen of bleating sheep and didn't answer me.

When we were far enough away from the wood-turning pole for me to hear him, he said we would probably find Wuffa in the Great Hall.

'Wuffa's one of the thanes. He's the chief thane, with Aesc away – he's the one to talk to you,' Penda said.

I worked out from this that Aesc was some kind of leader, and Wuffa his deputy.

'So Aesc, he's like the, the, the *mayor* of Haegelisdun?' I said.

Penda looked doubtful. 'You must have different words for things in Gipeswic,' he said. 'Aesc's the ealdorman. He owes allegiance to King Edmund and no one else.'

We walked round a pond seething noisily with ducks and past a long, low building which had foul, stinking steam escaping from the doorway.

'Dyeing shed. Don't breathe in,' Penda said.

He pointed to another wooden structure, bigger than the others, and with what looked like a double door at one end.

'And there's the Great Hall. Wuffa'll be in there. I'll take you.'

But before we reached the doors, they opened, and a man with a dark beard came out.

'Ah. There he is,' Penda said.

It struck me that he sounded nervous, and when I glanced at him, I saw he had the bright, eager expression of a person anxious not to offend someone they were a bit scared of. It was a look I recognised. Tracy used to look like that when Dean – who'd had Anger Issues – was living with us. Anything not to cause annoyance.

But Dean had been a weedy little rat of a man, and Wuffa was a different type altogether.

He wasn't particularly tall, but he was stocky and powerful. And he didn't look like he'd just been dragged through a hedge like Penda did – and everyone else I'd seen in the village. He was wearing what looked like a furry rug over one shoulder, but it didn't occur to me to think it looked ridiculous. It looked like it was meant to be there. And his tunic and leggings, although the same shape as Penda's, were decorated around the edges with little darts of sewing in a kind of silvery thread, and they weren't the colour of mud but vibrant red and green. Tied to his side was a long metal sword.

I'd seen films and TV shows where people run about shouting and slashing at each other with weapons very like the one hanging at Wuffa's side, but on the screen, you know it isn't real – there's always exciting music, lots of fake blood, shouting, and the clang of metal on metal. Close-up shots of gritted teeth, and heroic expressions. Wuffa's sword hung next to him like it was part of him, everyday and unremarkable, but still capable of slicing you in two like a piece of fruit.

It was a whole lot more frightening, if you want to know the truth.

'Who are you?' he asked.

'His name's Joss. He's from Gipeswic, that's why he looks different,' Penda said.

Wuffa's eyes were blank and dark and boring holes in me.

'We're suspicious of strangers, Joss from Gipeswic,' he said, 'and so would you be if you were us. Four years of Danish pirates helping themselves to anything they want, and those village scum on the other side of the river aren't much better.'

He spat viciously onto the ground between us.

'Are you a freeman or a slave?'

That riled me. I know that when you live on the Whitehorse estate, and your mother is Tracy, they'll use all sorts of words for you. Disadvantaged. Vulnerable. Distaste disguised as concern. Feckless. Chaotic.

I knew all that, but *slave*. It's a terrible word. A word dripping with ugliness from the time when people who looked more or less like me were traded like cattle. Slave! I am nobody's slave.

'A free man,' I said.

'And why are you here?'

His eyes had no expression in them at all. Life in this strange and vivid dream world, I suddenly realised, was cheap. Wuffa was standing beside me with his hand resting casually on the hilt of his sword, and I had better have a very good reason for being here.

And then I remembered Alice and her hand slipped confidingly through my arm. She'd said something about the Vikings. If only I could remember what it was. The muscles of Wuffa's face didn't move. His eyes on me were dispassionate, like I was an insect he was deciding whether or not to crush.

'I've got a message. From...'

From Alice. From Mr Richards.

'A message about the Vikings. They're on their way here. To...to rape and pillage. To conquer you.'

I stuttered into silence. The only other thing I could remember was the silly story Alice had told me, about the bridge, and there wasn't any way I could tell Wuffa that. He made a face of disgust.

'Those Danish pirates,' he said again. 'They came up the Waveney four years ago. And the year before, they laid waste the land between Gipeswic and the sea. We weren't ready for them then, but we are now.'

He turned round to go back into the hall.

'Where do you go to now, Joss?' Penda said.

I made another enormous effort to get free from the dream, but it was no good. I suddenly felt exhausted.

'I don't know. I don't have anywhere. I don't have a home any more,' I said.

I saw Wuffa go still for a second, his hand on the handle of the door.

'He can stay here tonight,' he said, 'Aesc will want to see him anyway.'

And then, without turning round, he went into the

Great Hall and banged the door behind him.

A small storm of giggling erupted. I hadn't noticed them before, but there was a crowd of children behind me, dirty faces and tangled hair and all of them laughing their heads off.

'What are they laughing at?'

There was a smile tugging at Penda's mouth, like someone who's too polite to laugh at you out loud.

'It's just you, I think,' he said. 'They've never seen anyone like you before.'

'They don't have to laugh,' I said. Although actually I didn't mind; it's hard to mind the sound of children laughing.

Penda grinned. 'I know where you can sleep tonight,' he said. 'She's a widow, she lost her son last month. She'll be glad to have someone to look after again. Come with me, and I'll introduce you.'

He wheeled the bike away, saying he would take great care of it.

CHAPTER FOUR

❀

fyrenðearfe
need for fire (literal translation)

COMFORT

❀

M y new foster carer looked at me suspiciously.
'Joss. That's a funny name,' she said.
'Yeah. And I don't think I've ever met
anyone called Cyneburga before, either,' I said.

Cyneburga's house was one room, filled with wood
smoke from a fire burning on some flat stones in the
middle of the room. There wasn't a chimney, just a hole in
the roof above the fireplace. The smoke stung my eyes. It
was a bit like being back on the Whitehorse estate, except
the smoke had a different, sort of outdoors-y smell. And,
unusually, my chest didn't feel tight at all.

My new foster carer was a stout, dumpy woman, with

long grey hair done in two plaits. She waved towards a low
stool covered in some sort of animal skin.

'Sit down, Joss. Are you hungry?'

I realised I was.

'Yes, please. What's Penda going to do with my bike? It
doesn't belong to me,' I said.

'Doesn't it? Are you a thief, then?' she asked.

'No,' I said, 'I borrowed it, that's all.'

Cyneburga made a hmm noise and turned to stir
something in the black pot that hung over the fire on a
tripod arrangement. Something in her quick, deft stirring
movements reminded me of Cressida and Tim, cooking
their garlicky creations in the enormous warm kitchen
with the sofa.

To my surprise and horror, I felt a sob building in my
throat. What was I *doing* here? I wanted home, and Ipswich.
I wanted the kitchen at Hoxne and the cooker that roasted
you alive in the summer. I was trapped in the Anglo-Saxon
past, in the middle of a mad dream I couldn't wake up
from. I was helpless. Helpless and trapped, and I had no
choice but to go along with it and see what happened next.

'Don't worry,' Cyneburga said, 'Aesc will sort things out
for you. It'll be all right, Joss.' She spoke gruffly, as if it
were a weakness to say anything kind.

'Yeah, all right,' I said.

'And here's your porridge,' she added.

I'd had porridge before, when the twins were babies just
learning to eat soft stuff and Tracy was going through one
of her phases of trying her hardest to be a Good Mother.

The packet it'd come in had been bright orange and had a picture of smiling kids waving spoons, and we'd eaten it with so much golden syrup the sugar set our teeth aching.

This was nothing like that.

It was grey and lumpy, and there were seeds that stuck in my teeth. And it was full of vegetables. I found bits of leek and onion and what I thought must be peas, as well as some purplish chunks I couldn't identify and some stringy bits that could have been anything.

I am not normally enthusiastic about vegetables or grey, lumpy porridge. But it must have been good because I ate everything in my bowl in under a minute.

'Eat, eat, eat. That's all you young folk do,' said Cyneburga, in the same grumbling tone she used for everything she said. She was like a person permanently at the end of their tether, although I couldn't see what she had to be so wound up about. At the same time, irrationally, she was dumping more of the grey gloop in my bowl.

'And I expect you're tired. You look tired, though God knows why, in the middle of the day. Young people are so lazy these days. It isn't just me who says it, either.'

I realised I was tired.

And probably lazy too, because I remember Tracy saying more or less exactly the same thing.

Cyneburga fussed around getting blankets out of a wooden chest and made up a bed on a low stand thing in the corner of the room.

The bed was hard as a rock, with a straw-stuffed pillow, and the blankets were made of thick scratchy stuff, but

I was so worn out I could have slept standing up. And my headache was coming back, in a tight, stabbing band around my head.

I closed my eyes. When I woke up this puzzling, detailed dream would be gone, and I'd be lying in a heap at the bottom of the quarry, next to a mangled bike. With a broken shoulder, probably. I drifted off to sleep totally convinced of it.

However.

When I opened my eyes what I actually found was a dark room and the fire on its flat stone fireplace almost out. It was night, because through the glassless window-shapes in the wall I could see the pinpricks of stars against a navy sky. A bulky shape came out of the darkness and spoke to me.

'Awake at last. I don't know how you can bear to sleep the clock round. I know I couldn't bear to be so lazy. Everyone tells me I work too hard, but I can't help it. I'm made that way. "You'll work yourself to a shadow, Cyneburga," they say. But I can't stop myself.'

She twitched the animal-skin blanket off me.

'Hurry up. Aesc wants to see you. He said to come as soon as you woke up.'

The dream, or concussion, or whatever it was, was continuing in all its weird, detailed glory. You don't normally smell dreams, or taste them, but I could smell the damp night air and the sour-sweet stink of the animals drifting in from outside. And the seeds from the tea-time porridge were still stuck between my teeth.

I slid my legs out from under the scratchy blankets.

'Wait! You can't go anywhere in those filthy garments. If that's what they're wearing in Gipeswic, heaven preserve me from ever going there. Here, let me get you something of my Eadwig's. You look to be something of the same size.'

She lit a candle from the ashes of the fire, and a yellow darting glow lit up the room enough for me to see her drop the soft pile of clothes onto the foot of my bed.

I put them on gingerly: some more peculiar tights and the same kind of shapeless tunic Penda had been wearing. They weren't all that different from what I'd been wearing anyway, but I understood that to Cyneburga the fact that my clothes came from a different place made them automatically foreign and strange. And 'filthy', although, again, there wasn't much difference there either. I wondered if they'd been washed since Eadwig died. I wondered if he'd died wearing them. I wondered, come to think of it, what he had died *of*.

'There. You look a bit more normal now,' Cyneburga said.

She took me by the wrist and towed me through the sleeping village, which was just as well because my eyes hadn't adjusted to the deep black of Haegelisdun at night, and I would probably have fallen right into the pond or walked into the pigsty.

It isn't real. It isn't real. It isn't real.

I said it over and over in my mind in time with my steps and the thudding of my heart.

But it felt real. I stepped on a cowpat in the darkness, and there was nothing dreamlike about that. The crisp surface, its delicate cracking and the soft ooze were as real as anything had ever been.

'Here. The Great Hall. Aesc and his thanes are inside,' Cyneburga said. She picked up a rock from the ground and hammered it against the double doors.

The noise from inside was the kind of Saturday-night roar of music and laughing that you hear when you walk past a pub or if someone's having a party. It didn't die down, but there was the sound of footsteps coming nearer.

'Are you…aren't you coming in with me?'

'Aesc doesn't want me; it's you he wants to see. Mind your manners. Don't forget to bend the knee.'

The door opened, and she stepped into the shadows and was gone.

I was on my own.

It was like those scenes in old cowboy movies when the stranger walks into the bar.

The singing and music stopped as abruptly as when you turn off a radio. And every face was turned towards me, a sea of strangers. Thirty, forty men maybe. (They were all men.) And a fire like the one at Cyneburga's, only this one was the kind of thing you'd build on a village green to burn a guy on. There were long tables arranged in three sides of a square around the fire, and the strange faces turned towards me were flickering orange in the firelight.

I'd obviously arrived in the middle of dinner because there was a mess of plates and jugs and the carcasses of chickens and things scattered over the tables.

A dog as big as a wolf stalked across the room towards me, its hackles up in a spiky ridge all down its back. Its teeth were showing.

'Call your dog off,' I said. It was meant to be a snapped order, but it came out as a squeak.

A blast of laughter hit me. The dog, or maybe it actually was a wolf – it looked dangerous enough – bared its teeth a bit more.

And then someone sitting at the far end of the table nearest the fire stood up.

'He's right. It isn't courteous to threaten a guest with dogs. Call off your cur, Aldred, and keep it under control.'

He beckoned to me.

'And you, stranger, you must be Joss. Approach the fire, come. Have meat and drink with us.'

He made room for me on the bench and pushed away a used plate covered in chicken bones.

'I'm Aesc, ealdorman of this shire. And these are my thanes, my brother warriors. You've met Wuffa, I think?'

I hadn't noticed before, but Wuffa was sitting on his left. I noticed as well that he was looking at me with as much hatred as if I'd just spat in his beer, or whatever it was that had been in the huge swirly patterned cup in front of him. And that he was drunk. He was one of those people whose faces give them away when they drink too much – he was flushed dark red and sweating, and his skin seemed to have swollen, so that the dark eyes had shrunk to pinpricks.

'Yeah. Hello, Wuffa. Nice to see you again,' I said.

'Wuffa told me the message you brought. About the Danish pirates being on their way. You must have travelled through a lot of hostile country between Gipeswic and Haegelisdun to deliver it, and I thank you for your courage.'

He had no idea exactly how far I'd come, but then neither did I.

'Here, have some mead. Let me pour some for you... try this.'

I swallowed some, and my eyes watered.

'How do you find it?'

The truthful reply would have been 'completely disgusting' so I answered diplomatically.

'I've never tasted anything like it in my life,' I said.

'The women brew it in the village. It has a taste all its own; you're right.'

He hacked me off some pieces of meat from a joint sitting on a plate in a pool of its own fat.

'Eat. We're famous for our hospitality in Haegelisdun,' he said.

I wasn't all that hungry because I was still full of Cyneburga's porridge, but I ate some to be polite. You had to take enormous mouthfuls because no one seemed to have a knife, only forks.

I liked Aesc. He had a gentle way of speaking that reminded me of someone, only I couldn't think who.

The thing was, I still didn't *believe* any of this. It's like when something terrible happens – you know it's true but you don't believe it. Last year I'd sat in a corridor outside an A and E resuscitation room while they pumped out all the crap from Tracy's stomach. I'd sat there for two hours waiting for someone to come out and tell me whether she would live or die. It had been the same then – a disconnected feeling of just not believing it was happening to you. Like watching yourself on TV. And the other thing about being in the middle of not quite believing what's going on is that you notice things, every little detail. You're sensitive as litmus paper. The wall by my chair in the A and E corridor had peeled and cracked with damp into a complicated pattern of circles and criss-crossing lines – I could have *drawn* it afterwards.

It was the same now; I noticed everything with this kind of extra intensity, like I'd been given X-ray glasses. I noticed the way Aesc's fine, faded hair crowded in at his temples, and the web of tired lines around his eyes. I noticed the starburst pattern of the spilt gravy and chicken bones on the table by my elbow. And then I noticed something else. Over Aesc's shoulder, just out of the splash of the firelight, I saw a girl walking along the edges of the hall towards a kind of curtained alcove at the back.

She walked quickly and easily in the shadows, then slipped through the curtains with a small swish of the long, dark dress she was wearing. She was carrying a young child in her arms, a younger brother or sister, I guessed. It was only a few seconds, but I liked her. I liked the confident straightness of her back and the air she had of belonging utterly. It was more than that, actually; it was almost like

I recognised her. I felt – I knew it was impossible but I felt it – somehow like I'd been looking for her without my knowing it, and that I'd finally found her. Watching the curtain close behind her, like water closing over a thrown stone, I felt a soft pluck at my heart.

'She's my daughter,' Aesc said, seeing my eyes follow her, 'she's called Merwenna. And that's my son with her. Godfrey.'

I made an indeterminate noise. My mouth was full of meat anyway, so I couldn't have said anything.

'Fride, my wife, died in childbed two winters ago,' Aesc said, 'Merwenna is my greatest support. I don't know what I'd have done without her these last two years.'

He put his hand on my shoulder.

'Your message is timely. We've had years of lightning raids by those Norse animals. Every month or so they come, then they get back in their damned boats and go back across the whale road. They're a constant danger. We have to be on our guard continually.'

He drank some of the disgusting sweet mead.

'We knew it was only a matter of time before they launched a proper attack.'

I swallowed down a big, scratchy lump of chicken.

'I don't know why I'm here,' I said. I hadn't planned to say it, it just popped out.

Aesc smiled a tired sort of smile. 'Well. You never know, perhaps you were sent from heaven to warn us. Perhaps that's why.'

Out of the corner of my eye, I could see Wuffa's flushed,

angry face. It was clear that heaven was the last place he thought I'd come from.

It was Rufus Palmier-Thompson all over again. Some people can't stand the sight of a stranger. They can't bring themselves to trust them. It's easier to hate them, and stamp on them like you would stamp on an ant.

I didn't have long to wait.

The food was all finished, but it looked like the drinking was going to carry on all night. I moved away from the fire and watched a group of men playing a complicated game with dice, trying to understand the rules.

Someone gripped me painfully on my shoulder and pulled me off the bench I was sitting on.

It was Wuffa.

'You are a lying piece of scum,' he said.

He spat the words out like cherry stones.

'A lying, devious piece of Gipeswic shit.'

I don't take that kind of talk from anybody. Wuffa and his rage might only be the results of concussion, the by-products of fizzing electrical brain activity, but still, I don't take that kind of talk from anyone.

'Let go of my bloody arm,' I said.

I wrenched myself free. 'And don't talk to me like that. I've done nothing to piss you off. I can't help it if you're a…a xenophobe.'

He wasn't listening. He started shouting before I'd

finished speaking, shouting that I was a piece of lying scum and that everything I'd said about having a message for Aesc about the Norsemen had been a lie.

'I know what you are. You're a dirty spy. You've been sent here to…'

'Yeah, that's right, I'm spying. I'm counting how many bloody geese and cows you have, like that's really important.'

We were both properly shouting by now, and people were looking round. The twangy, harp-like music that somebody had been playing trailed off, and the hum of noisy talk shrank to a small, anxious murmur.

He pushed me in my chest, and I staggered back. And then he drew out a sword and held it steadily, pointing fifteen centimetres away from my face.

I looked round for Aesc, but he was nowhere to be seen. It was pointless in any case; he wasn't a friendly teacher who would sort out a playground spat. Life here was, I had already realised, cheap.

'I haven't got a sword. Not exactly fair, is it?' I said.

My voice shook. Breathe, breathe.

'No, you don't have a sword because you are a nothing. A son of the soil. A filthy, spying slave.'

He took a step towards me. The metal edges of the sword caught the firelight and glinted.

Another man spoke up. 'Here, whatever your name is. Joss. You can borrow mine. Its name is Bloodworm.'

A sword with a name. But it was meant kindly, so I muttered 'thank you', and picked the thing up with both hands.

It was much heavier than I'd expected, and it took all my strength just to hold it up. And the hilt and handle were carved into curly patterns, so it wasn't all that easy to hold anyway.

Wuffa swung his arms around his head, and I tensed, waiting for the blow. It smashed down against the blade of my borrowed sword. I felt my bones vibrate with the shock of it, and nearly fell. He wound his arms around again, and this time I couldn't get out of the way in time. A quick, shocking pain sliced through my arm, and when I looked down there was a long rent in Eadwig's tunic, welling with my own dark red blood.

It was the pain that made it clear. You don't imagine pain like that.

I didn't believe in time travel, in reincarnation, or any of that New-Age bullshit that Tracy and her loser friends talk about. Crystals and angel cards. I didn't believe in any of it. I knew that none of it was true.

But whether or not I believed in it, it had *happened*.

Wuffa was coming nearer with his sword in his hand and a sort of fierce joy in his eyes. I was going to be cut in two. I was going to die. I didn't feel frightened, only profoundly sad. Wuffa's next slash at me would be the end; my life was about to be over, and it didn't feel like it had properly begun.

◎◎

CHAPTER FIVE

❦

læce-feoh
leech-fee (literal translation)

DOCTOR

❦

And then, another voice over all the clamour. Someone was pushing his way to the front of the knot of men gathered to watch us, he walked up to me, hands up and palms out in a 'stop' gesture.

'Stop it, Wuffa, this is murder. This is a man against a boy. If you want to fight, I'll fight you.'

The speaker was taller and looked older than me – late teens or maybe early twenties – with fair hair and a pleasant musical voice. He had the kind of cheekbones that stick out beneath the skin, giving him an angular look.

'Get out of the way, Leofric. I've got no quarrel with you,' Wuffa said.

The young man next to me laughed. 'That's rubbish, Wuffa. You quarrel with everyone. Come on, I'll fight you if you want to fight.'

He took the sword off me, and I pressed my hand into the bleeding cut in my arm. I was bleeding a *lot*. And it hurt.

Leofric leant towards me, his eyes fixed on Wuffa.

'Go through into the bower.' He indicated where he meant with a jerk of his head. 'Merwenna's inside, she'll put something on your wound.'

Merwenna: like Cyneburga, not a name I'd ever heard before this evening, but – unlike Cyneburga, which was an ugly word full of lumps and sharp edges – beautiful and soft on your tongue. *Merwenna*: three little descending syllables, like something small and solid falling downstairs.

She was sitting on the bed with the child on her knee; she seemed to be searching through his hair for something, but when I came in, she stopped and looked up.

'Umm...Leofric said to come and find you. I'm bleeding,' I said.

She slid the child off her lap and stood up.

'So you are,' she said.

What Leofric had called the bower was really like a little bedroom, with a low bed, a wooden chest and a kind of rack for clothes. There were rushes on the floor, like in the hall, but these ones smelled nice, like pine. And there was a colourful rug beside the bed, which made it more homely. On the other side of the curtain, you could hear the clashes of Wuffa and Leofric fighting. But inside it felt calm and cut off and peaceful.

She helped me slip the tunic up and off over my head. I could think of nothing whatever to say to her as she bent her head to look closely at the scarlet slash on my arm.

'I've got something that'll help it heal,' she said, 'and some bandages. Wait here with Godfrey. I won't be long.'

I didn't like to sit down on the bed and there wasn't anywhere else, so I stood in the middle of the little room, feeling suddenly exposed and foolish without a top on. Godfrey stared at me with the frank, unpretending gaze of the very young.

'Hello,' I said.

He didn't say anything, so I winked and stuck out my tongue to make him smile. I am not afraid of small children, like some people are, because I've been used to the twins. He slipped off the bed and toddled over to me. I crouched down so we were at the same level.

'Hello, you.'

I judged the child to be not more than two. He pressed against me, warm and damp and smelling like a young animal. I crossed my eyes and stuck out my tongue again, and he gave a short, bubbly laugh.

The curtain parted, and Merwenna came back in, carrying a bowl of water and some other stuff in a basket.

'Get away from him, Godfrey. You'll get blood all over you,' she said. I couldn't tell if she was annoyed or not.

'Sorry. I didn't want him to miss you and get upset,' I said.

Merwenna took a piece of material and began to wipe the blood from my arm. She wiped carefully and quickly, and then squeezed out the cloth into the bowl. The blood curled through the water like smoke.

'Godfrey's your brother,' I said, not quite a question.

'Yes. Sometimes I love him; sometimes he drives me mad.'

She peeled a lid made of what looked like goatskin from a jar and spread a thin layer of pale green paste across my cut.

'I've got two sisters. I feel like that too sometimes. Ow! That stings. What's in that stuff?'

'It's called stime. Made from watercress. Keep still while I bandage.'

I tried not to wince.

'Who's the knight in shining armour out there?'

'What do you mean?'

'The man in the hall, the one fighting Wuffa. Leofric. Who is he? Why'd he do me such a favour?'

There was a crash outside, as if someone had fallen over the bench. There was a buzz of laughter and voices, so I guessed the fighting was over.

After a second or two, the harp or whatever it was started playing again.

'Oh,' Merwenna said, 'I don't think Leofric was actually doing you a favour – he just likes fighting. He's as bad as Wuffa in his way. Only not so bad-tempered.' An unconscious edge of softness had crept into her voice.

'I hope he's OK,' I said.

Her face was centimetres from mine. Her brow was furrowed and her mouth slightly pursed as she concentrated on bandaging my arm. It was an expression I recognised; Tracy made the same face doing up the twins' coats.

'He'll be all right,' Merwenna said.

She finished bandaging and straightened up.

'There. It might feel a bit tight, but it's got to be, to stop the bleeding.'

Her skin was that thin, pale kind you can see the veins through. She was about half a head shorter than I was.

'It's fine,' I said.

I picked up my tunic top from the bed.

'Don't put it back on,' Merwenna said, 'let me mend it. I'll just take Godfrey to his nurse first. He should've been in bed hours ago.'

She took the boy and went out. The room seemed suddenly empty, now she was no longer in it, and I was aware again of standing there half-naked, in only Eadwig's baggy and peculiar trousers. I thought about putting the tunic back on and slipping away.

But before I could do it, the curtain twitched, and Leofric came into the bower. He was out of breath and there was a sheen of sweat on his face, but he was grinning as though it had all been a great joke.

'Well that's all over,' he said. 'Wuffa's got the need to fight someone out of his system for another day. God in heaven! I'll be sorry for the Norsemen when he gets at them.'

He flopped down on the bed.

'Um...thanks. I'm Joss by the way,' I said.

'We know that, Joss, my father told us. And you don't need to thank him,' Merwenna said, 'He likes fighting. What fools men are.'

I hadn't heard her come in. She sat down next to Leofric,

and he put his arm around her.

Merwenna started to stitch the tear in Eadwig's tunic, using a needle that looked like it was made of bone. I noticed her face had softened around the eyes and mouth.

'Talking of your father, hadn't we better go and leave him in peace? He'll want the bower to himself, and it's getting late,' Leofric said.

'Yes, he will,' Merwenna said, 'and I'm tired too. You'd better take Joss back to Mistress Cyneburga, Leofric; he'll never find his way in the dark.'

'No, I won't,' I said. I had never known how dark night was until now. I mean, I'd known in theory, but when you could switch on a light or flick on a torch, the darkness never seemed very real, somehow. Not like here, where the blackness was so complete it made no difference whether your eyes were open or closed.

'All right. She'll be glad to put you up tonight. It's only a month or so since Eadwig died, so she'll be pleased to have someone to fuss round again.'

'She didn't sound very pleased,' I said, thinking of the red face and low continuous grumbling.

Leofric laughed and said it was just her way.

We left the hall – there was no sign of Wuffa, and the crowd had thinned and quietened – and threaded our way through the village.

'How's the arm?' Leofric asked cheerfully. He was always cheerful. I thought that he must be one of those people who find it easy to be happy.

'It feels a bit better, actually. Merwenna put some sort of

cream on it,' I said.

'She's clever with herbs and things,' Leofric said. He said it with a careless pride that made it easy to tell how much he loved her.

'Is Merwenna your girlfriend?' I asked.

'My...oh, I see. I don't really know, but she's in my heart. It's like she's part of me.'

If anyone on the Whitehorse estate had ever said that about anybody, there would have been howls of mockery. In fact, you could never imagine – not in a million years – anyone on the Whitehorse estate saying anything so cringey.

Only it didn't sound cringey when Leofric said it. It sounded heartfelt and ordinary and true.

'Are you...is your father one of Aesc's thanes?' I asked.

'He was,' Leofric said, 'and they were good friends as well. As close as he is now to Wuffa. Mind those beehives. You don't want to knock one of those over in the dark.'

'Is he dead?' I asked. Hardly anyone I knew had a father – not in the sense of living in the same house and seeing them every day – but I didn't know anyone whose father had actually died.

'Killed in a skirmish two years ago. Fighting next to Aesc. I live with my cousins,' Leofric said.

'Against the Norsemen, do you mean?' I said.

'No,' Leofric said, 'against the scum from the other side of the river.'

The contemptuous way he said it set up faint echoes in my mind. I'd heard something like this before. Then I got it: Tracy talking about the people from the Grange

Wood estate (and, probably, the people from Grange Wood talking about us).

'Here we are, Joss. Cyneburga's house. I'll say goodnight,' Leofric said.

I felt for the door handle. 'Goodnight, Leofric. See you in the morning,' I said.

Because I would. I knew it now. I didn't begin to understand how or why, but falling into that quarry in Hoxne had sent me out of my own time and landed me here. It had happened. Leofric and Merwenna were as real as I was. I would go to sleep in Cyneburga's house, and I would wake up there tomorrow.

The front door was opened, an upended rectangle of bright pale light against the gloom. My back was stiff from the hard bed and my feet ached from the shoes I'd worn yesterday – Eadwig's shoes, which were really thick, leathery socks tied up with twine. My arm throbbed, and the bandage had stiffened in the night with blood.

'What's that noise?'

The doorway was filled with a substantial silhouette.

'Awake at last. Come and have some breakfast, Joss. I've gone to the trouble of making it, so you might as well eat it.'

I dragged the scratchy wool blanket off the bed and wrapped it round me. I was only wearing Eadwig's leggings and the morning air was cool.

'What's that noise?' I asked again.

I could hear, over the squawks of poultry, a sound of female sobbing and an undercurrent of anxious chatter. It was coming, I thought, from behind the pigpen, beside the hut next door to Cyneburga's.

'I don't know,' said Cyneburga, 'but you can't go out like that...come back, Joss! You aren't decent!'

Decent, hah! You see more flesh than I was displaying every summer Saturday on the beach at Felixstowe. I ignored her and went round the next-door hut.

A small knot of people had gathered, as people cluster around the scene of an accident. They were getting in the way; some of the women had pressed their hands to their mouths. I pushed my way to the front and saw Merwenna and Godfrey.

She was kneeling on the ground, and he was slumped against her shoulder. She was shaking him.

'Breathe, Godfrey...please breathe. Oh God in heaven, please. He can't breathe...'

He flopped against her like a bag of wet washing. He had turned a pale bluish colour and his lips were stretched, snatching in air in little gasps.

I knelt down next to her.

'What's happening?' I asked.

Her face was blurred with crying, like a watercolour in the rain.

'It's the worms,' she said, 'worms in his chest. Every so often they attack him, but it's never been this bad before. Leofric's gone to get the physician, but he can't breathe.'

I held onto her shoulders and made her look at me.

'He'll be all right. And it isn't worms. Stay here, I'll be back in a minute.'

I plunged through the little group of watching villagers, and back to Cyneburga's.

'Where's my bike, Cyneburga?'

'Mistress Cyneburga to you. And if you mean the little cart thing, Wuffa has care of it. It's not for the likes of you, because you're a son of a pig with no manners.'

I ignored her and headed for the door.

'Where's Wuffa put it? I need something from the saddlebag…quick, Cyneburga. It's urgent.'

Cyneburga stood in the doorway, a pillar box with arms, pointing a spoon at me fiercely.

'In the Great Hall. I imagine. Because it's a new thing; important… Don't you go and try to take it back or he'll cut you in half, and I for one won't stop him.'

'I'm not going to *take* it,' I said.

I ran past her, out of the house, and around the pigpen. The Great Hall was easy to find in the daylight, and I headed towards it, clutching the blanket around my shoulders like Superman's cape, dodging the dogs that ran with me, barking, as if it was a game. Tim's bike was leaning against the wall, beside the open door. Also leaning against the wall was a teenage boy with a dirty face and hair in pigtails.

'You! Get away from that…Wuffa's orders. No one to touch it. Keep your hands off!'

'Calm down. I'm not going to take it,' I said. I unzipped the little bag behind the saddle, felt around inside and found my inhalers.

☯

When I returned, Godfrey was the same pale blue colour, and seemed even less conscious than he had thirty seconds before. He flopped against Merwenna's shoulder, and his head was lolling forward like it was too heavy for his neck. And then Leofric was beside me, panting like he'd run a long way. He had a grey-haired man with him who was carrying a pottery bottle under each arm.

'It's the physician,' Leofric said.

The man with grey hair (yes, I thought, he does look like a doctor) uncorked the bottles and set them down next to Godfrey, who was making a hooting, wheezing sound as he tried to breathe.

'What's in those mixtures?'

He looked at me like one of the pigs had jumped out of the sty and spoken to him.

'In this one, hare-hune boiled with water, sweetened with honey. In this one, essence of nettle. Both are effective cures for worms in the chest.'

Oh, excellent.

'Wait a minute. Let me try this first,' I said.

I flipped the cap off the Ventolin.

'Godfrey, breathe in through your mouth,' I said.

I held the nozzle of the inhaler to his lips, waited for the whistle of his in-drawn breath, and squeezed the trigger.

Please let it not be empty.

And please let it work.

And please let me be right – maybe it wasn't an asthma attack at all. Maybe it really was an attack of worms in the chest. Maybe hare-hune and nettles were *exactly* what was needed.

'Godfrey, breathe for God's sake.'

I squeezed the Ventolin again, and its sour chemical smell floated to me above the smell of the pigpen.

He took a great gasping breath.

And then another one.

A faint flush of pink broke through the pallor.

'Come on, Godfrey.'

The slit eyes opened, and the small body shuddered.

'Pass me the other one, will you Merwenna? The brown one,' I said. I gave him a couple of squirts of the brown inhaler, just for luck.

It was like magic. I had never noticed it before, but it was a sort of miracle how things worked. And it never occurred to you to think about it, you just accepted it. Ventolin; food arriving every day on the shelves at the supermarket; the Internet. You had no idea how, but it all just happened. There was so much I didn't understand.

'Oh, Leofric, Joss. It's working, it's working. He's better, he's breathing again! Oh, God in heaven, thank God in heaven.'

She scrambled to stand up, her little brother in her arms. Leofric curled his arm around her shoulder; and I was suddenly aware that somewhere on the mad dash to the Great Hall and back, the scratchy blanket had slipped off me and that I was squatting in the dust in only Eadwig's grubby leggings. I stood up; exposed as an X-ray, and Cyneburga came huffing into view, with the ratty blanket dragging from her fingers in the breeze like a flag.

The doctor corked his bottles again, and glared at me. Oh good, someone else in Haegelisdun who hated my guts.

'This is witchcraft,' he said. He said it quietly, but there was a world of venom behind the words. His eyes were hard with suspicion.

I straightened up. The villagers, who had gathered around helplessly watching when Godfrey had been gasping for breath, were all now looking at me, and their faces had gone still and watchful.

'It's medicine, not witchcraft,' I said. 'It's…it's the kind of medicine we use in Gipeswic. Look, it worked, didn't it? It's new to you, but that doesn't make it wrong, does it?'

I held his unblinking gaze until he dropped his eyes. I didn't think I had convinced him, not for a moment, but at least the glaring had stopped. One of the villagers patted my bare shoulder, and the touch felt suddenly friendly.

'I'm going to take Godfrey home. Come with me, Leofric,' Merwenna said.

I felt her warm hand on my other arm.

'Thank you, Joss.'

I watched her go. Cyneburga draped the blanket over me again, and I went with her round the pigpen and back to her house. My skin was still fizzing where Merwenna had touched it.

෨෨

ChAPTER SIX

❧

bréost-aswille
heart swell (literal translation)

LOVE

❧

A esc had come to find me later that morning, and said I was to make Haegelisdun my home for as long as I wanted.

'Godfrey is my only son. And the only one I'm likely to have,' he said. He didn't make a big thing of saying it, parading his sadness in front of you the way some people do; he just said it.

'I don't know if Aethelred and his potions and chanting would've made a difference, but anyway, they weren't needed. Godfrey's breathing fine now, and it's thanks to you.'

'That's all right,' I said. It sounded a bit stupid, but I

didn't know what else to say.

'Do you mind having a lodger, Mistress Cyneburga?' Aesc said.

Cyneburga said she was sure I'd be no trouble at all. She said it so doubtfully that I wanted to laugh.

'Thank you very much,' I said, 'I *would* like to stay here for a while, if you're sure it's all right.'

Aesc said he was glad. When he smiled, the lines around his eyes and mouth deepened and crinkled so that he looked ancient, only he couldn't have been all that old, if he was Godfrey's father. People here looked older than they were anyway; Penda, with his leathery skin and blackened teeth and the skinny rat tails of his hair, looked like a battered, elderly tramp, but I bet he wasn't more than thirty.

'Of course it's all right. After what you did for Godfrey, Joss, it already feels like you belong here. Don't take any notice of Wuffa. He gets carried away sometimes.'

He turned to go, and then turned back.

'I think your coming is an omen. A good omen. I think you're going to make a big difference to us.'

This time he really did go.

'Just you and me now, Cyneburga,' I said.

So I was back in foster care again, only this time with Cyneburga in a wooden one-roomed hut with no toilet instead of with Cressida and Tim in the biggest house I'd seen in my life. Life in Haegelisdun didn't feel exactly normal, but I got used to it. The strangeness and shock wore off a little more each day.

Despite what she told Aesc, Cyneburga grumbled and

moaned all the time about the extra work I was causing her, but I liked to think it was just her way. She was like a lot of people; moaning about everything was her default setting.

'Come off it Cyneburga, I mean, Mistress Cyneburga. I must save you more trouble than I cause you. Look how many buckets of water I bring in for you, and the well's miles away. And I'm getting better at making bread.'

Merwenna had shown me the way bread was made. All you did was mix the grainy, gritty flour with water till you had a sticky lump, which you then stuck into the fire between two flat stones. It was easier than I'd thought.

'You wouldn't recognise hard work if it stabbed you in the eyes,' Cyneburga said, 'Holiday, holiday all the time.'

I remembered Tracy saying similar things.

Every time I thought of her, there was this hard little pain in my heart, but there was also a funny, warm feeling to think of women, all down the ages, complaining about the same kinds of things, using almost the same words and the same tone. It made me feel at home. And it was comforting to know that some things never changed.

'I'll *work*,' I said, 'just tell me what job you want me to do and I'll do it.'

'Not ploughing,' Leofric said. He'd come in with Merwenna to collect me for an afternoon's harvesting in the bean fields behind the village. 'You couldn't plough a straight line if your life depended on it.'

'And not making nettle ropes,' Merwenna said. 'The fuss you made about a few stings, it was beyond belief.'

When she laughed, it made you want to laugh as well, even though the joke was on you.

'Well, I don't know what we're going to do with you, Joss. By Aesc's good grace you've made a home with us, and you've been here a week and hardly lifted a finger.'

'I've baked bread,' I said. 'I baked every bit of bread we ate this week.'

'You can't make bread for the whole village,' Cyneburga said, 'and that last loaf you made would've broken every tooth in my head, if I'd had any to break.'

I felt indignant. I'd chopped wood and fetched water for a week. My spine was aching from the knobbly bit at the top to the bony bit at the bottom, my hands were cracked from gutting fish and raw from helping the children comb the wool before it was made into thread for clothes.

'I've *been* working,' I said.

'Come on, Joss,' Leofric said, 'beans don't pick themselves. Don't worry, Cyneburga. We'll look after him, and make sure he doesn't cut his hand off.'

In the end, we decided what I'd be best at was helping the women in the dyeing house.

Some of the village children stopped the sheep- and geese-minding to stare at me as I trooped towards the dyeing house in the middle of a crowd of women. I had that first-day-of-school feeling.

A clod of mud hit me squarely in the middle of my back.

'You little...'

They scattered delightedly, squealing and shrieking.

'Little sods,' I said.

I felt a hand plucking at my arm.

'Take no notice. Do you want to come with me? I can show you what to do, if you like.'

Her name, she told me, was Osthryd. She was one of those shapeless girls, thick-limbed and lumpily built. I was too boiling mad with the silly kids to be grateful to her for offering to help.

'Oh, all right,' I said.

Osthryd tucked an arm like a ham through mine.

'Come on, then,' she said. 'Oh, it's going to be fun! Everyone's looking forward to seeing you. No one's ever seen anyone from outside the village before. No one's ever seen anyone who looks like you. And it'll be a treat to have a man in the dyeing house.'

'God, don't you start,' I said.

Inside the dyeing house, it was jungle-hot and the smell made your eyes water.

I was worse than useless at first. There were piles of wool that you had to comb first, and then carry across to be spun and woven. The wool was straight off the sheep, rinsed only to get the worst of the dirt off. Waterlogged, it was heavy and greasy and matted into clumps; the combing took ages and split the skin around your fingers like millions of paper cuts. The children, with their nimble fingers, were much better at it than I was.

'You'll soon get the hang of it,' Osthryd said. A woman

called Ethelinda called out something rude and raucous across the dyeing house, and Osthryd flushed happily, a deep and ugly red. And when all the wool was combed, you carried it – still stinking and greasy – into the weaving shed to be spun and made into cloth. You could hardly see the hands of the weavers sitting at the looms, they moved so fast. Once all that was done, you could get on with dyeing the cloth.

The vats of pigment suspended over the fires smelled poisonous, and bubbled like the beakers in a mad-scientist movie. Most of the dyes were green or brown, because they were the easiest to make. Sometimes there would be a vat of reddish dye, but this was more difficult to make and took longer, so Aesc and the other thanes were the only ones who had red clothes.

Walking around in his colourful tunic with its stitched decoration and scalloped edges, as far apart from Penda and the other muddy scruffs as a peacock from a sparrow, Leofric exhibited a not-quite-pride I seemed to recognise. Yes, that was it: Danny Bird who'd lived two doors down on the Whitehorse estate, swaggering in his £200 trainers and new leather jacket. A cut above – Leofric, I mean, whose father had been a thane and friend of Aesc, not Danny Bird, whose father, like everyone else's, was gone with the wind, and whose mother worked part-time in the launderette and grew cannabis for schoolchildren in her airing cupboard.

The hot, vegetable smell of the dye got into my lungs and throat and stayed there. The liquid spat as I stirred it, and within an hour my arms were dotted with tiny burn marks.

'There's a way of stirring it that means you don't get burnt,' Osthryd said, 'Like this.'

Her hands rested on mine like flat, pale fish as she showed me what to do. There was another gale of laughter from the other dyers.

'They'll get used to you in time,' Osthryd said, 'it's just that we're not used—'

'Yeah, I know,' I said, 'but I hope they get used to me soon. I'm starting to feel like a pork pie in a famine.'

I didn't really mind it. It was mockery, but friendly mockery, and it made me feel sort of homely and as if they wanted me there.

And then after a week or two, it was like I'd worked there all my life. I still thought about home, the twins and Tracy, but only in the wistful half-sad way you remember games you used to play where you were young. What was real now was living with Cyneburga; getting up before it was light to go to work; the smell of outdoors and my own unwashed clothes, which I got used to after a while. Meals of grains and vegetables and flat, dense bread I got to like after a while. Apples and plums and another fruit called a medlar that was sour enough to leave your teeth squeaking. Fishing with Leofric, and teaching him and Merwenna how to ride a bike. In the evenings, lying around in the bower with the two of them, learning the complicated rules of their dice games.

All that was what was real now.

I knew that Hoxne and Tracy and Alice were real too, but they had become something I knew only in theory. Theoretical knowledge, nothing to do with now. Like, I knew the world was round but I didn't go around thinking about it all the time, and the knowledge didn't make any difference to me living my life: laughing till I almost choked when Leofric rode Tim's bike – which fascinated him – into a holly bush; working in the dyeing sheds with Osthryd.

Leofric poked his head round the dyeing-house door.

'Joss, are you nearly finished? I'm going fishing – it's a lovely evening.'

Something about the frail, unexpected word 'lovely' made my heart turn over.

'I'm not sure. Got a bit to do yet, I think,' I said.

The air was filled with birds singing behind him. My back ached from stirring the pots of foul, boiling dye all afternoon, and the stink of it had given me a headache.

Osthryd came bustling up from somewhere.

'Don't worry, Joss, I'll finish this pot,' she said. 'You go and fish with Leofric.'

'If you're sure,' I said.

After the hours in the dyeing house, I couldn't wait to breathe fresh air again.

'Thanks, Osthryd. See you tomorrow.'

⊚⊚

'You know what, Joss,' Leofric remarked as we walked through the village, 'you're definitely a hit with Osthryd. She was looking at you like she'd like to eat you. You'd better have this.'

He took something out of the pouch he wore slung round his waist and handed it to me.

'What is it?'

'It's a comb. Go on, take it. I've got another one.'

It didn't surprise me. I knew that Leofric was proud of his long, fair hair; at any rate, he was always fiddling with it to keep it neat. I took the little comb he gave me – it was made of animal bone, and had a curly, carved handle – and attempted without success to drive it through the matted tangles on my head.

'That's it! Make yourself look nice for Osthryd,' Leofric said.

I gave him a shove that knocked him against the chicken coop.

'I need combs with wider teeth. And do me a favour. Haven't you seen her face? It's like a potato,' I said.

'Like a what?' Leofric said.

I remembered about potatoes and Sir Walter Raleigh.

'Oh, you know. Pale and lumpy and ugly.'

Leofric laughed. I felt small and mean and cruel.

Down at the river, Leofric set up his fishing line – lines, I mean, because he had a clever system of several short lines hanging from one long one he strung across the river from trees on either bank.

'There must be so many fish in this river,' I said. That was something I'd noticed about Haegelisdun. There were more birds than I was used to, more bees and insects and wild animals like frogs and mice and foxes – creatures you never saw normally, at home. More moving, noisy, buzzing life.

'What? Yes, I suppose so,' Leofric said.

Setting up the lines had got us both soaked from the waist down, and we flopped on the sloping river bank in the sun to dry. The sky was so bright it was almost white. The heat would bake us dry in no time.

'Merwenna,' I said, 'she's your girlfriend, right?'

'You asked that before. Yes, in a way.'

His voice sounded thick and sleepy. He was one of those people who could fall asleep anywhere, I had found, like a cat in a patch of sunlight.

'What kind of a way?' I asked. It was like probing an aching tooth, a bit painful but impossible to resist.

'Well, we're not properly betrothed, not yet. But we will be soon. Maybe this summer.'

'*Betrothed*,' I said, trying out the word on my tongue like a piece of too-hot food. 'Aren't you both…isn't Merwenna a bit young for that?'

'We're not so young. She has sixteen summers, and I have nineteen. Anyway, what's the point of getting betrothed if you're old?'

I thought about Tracy, sixteen years old and me on the way. I thought of what her life must have been like, no more university plans or better days to come, only a soul-eroding constant shortage of money, and watching all the girls she'd been at school with get interesting jobs and move away.

'You're right, I suppose. Yeah. You're right,' I said.

He sat up.

'Come on, are you dry yet? Let's practise again on your...what is the word for it? I keep forgetting.'

'My bike. All right. Come on, then,' I said.

Aesc and some of the other thanes had been looking at the bike carefully, trying I suppose to figure out how the chain worked, and the gears. Which makes them sound like simpletons, only of course they weren't; I wouldn't know how a spaceship worked if one landed on the village green in Hoxne. Come to think about it, I didn't actually know how the gears on a bike worked. And like me, Leofric didn't seem interested in the mechanics, only in learning how to ride the thing.

The bike was just one activity. We did other stuff together, me and Leofric, and more often than not, Merwenna as well. The two of them tried to teach me to ride a horse, but I kept slipping off, and in the end I lost my nerve. And Merwenna showed me how to make bread that wasn't as hard as concrete. Or we would just go for walks away from the village, singing the same kind of songs about battles that Penda had tried to teach me. Walking about, making bread; it doesn't sound that special. But I didn't think I'd laughed so much before.

Leofric was determined to master cycling, but he was

terrible at first and kept falling off.

'What do you do, to keep upright?'

He aimed a pretend blow at Merwenna, who was laughing till the tears came because he'd just fallen off for the twentieth time.

'I don't know what I do. I just sit on it and pedal.' I said, 'Look, get back on. Back in the saddle.'

'Like you did, on the horse, you mean,' Leofric said, but he climbed back on the bike and I ran behind, holding onto the saddle to help him balance.

The bike jerked and bumped over the grass. I was panting, and my arm and shoulder were starting to hurt when quite suddenly he got it. I wasn't supporting him any more but just running along behind, and then he accelerated away from me, and down the hill, shouting with triumph and his tunic billowing out behind him like a flag.

Out of breath, I walked back up the hill to where Merwenna was waiting.

'Your turn next,' I said.

She grinned. Merwenna was the only girl I'd met in my life who even knew *how* to grin.

'The girls where you live,' she said, 'do they all ride bikes?'

I looked over at her. Her eyes were fixed on Leofric, whose triumphant roaring could still be heard from two fields away.

'Yeah, I suppose so. They all know how to, anyway, even if they don't actually do it,' I said.

'It must be very different in Gipeswic,' she said.

A tiny breeze stirred the long grass of the field. The silvery leaves of the trees either side of us made a shushing sound. On the opposite slope, some of the village children were looking after a scattered flock of dirty grey sheep.

'In a way it is. In lots of ways it's not all that different,' I said.

She said nothing.

'It's nice here,' I said, 'Haegelisdun. I like it.'

She snapped off the heads of some tall white flowers that were sticking up above the grass. The cuckoo-spit from the grass trailed across my hands and arms, making them sticky.

'I like it too. I mean, I think I do. But I don't know, not really, because I've never been anywhere else. So I can't compare.'

She was still smiling, watching Leofric pedal wildly along the dusty path of the bottom of the hill. He was utterly confident now, standing up to stamp on the pedals. He'd be shouting 'look no hands' in a minute.

But her voice sounded sad. Or not exactly sad, but something. Wistful.

'Have you even been to another country, Joss?' she asked, 'You know. Across the whale-road to a completely different place. Like the Norsemen.'

I didn't want to start telling her about the school trip to Calais in Year 8, so I just said, 'Yeah. Once,' and left it at that.

'God in heaven! You're so lucky, Joss,' she said, 'I can't imagine what it's like, to see everything so different. What's it like in the country of the Norsemen, do you know?'

My knowledge of Scandinavia was limited. And I wasn't even completely sure which country the Vikings had come from. So I told her about fjords and deep snow and ice and the Northern Lights. Digging deeper into my store of facts, I came up with reindeer and salt licks and mile upon mile of fir trees, and then I ran dry completely.

She clenched her fists into balls at her side.

'I can't believe I'll never see any of those things,' she said.

'I've never seen them either,' I said, 'I just know about them, that's all.'

She didn't reply. I got the feeling we'd gone further than we meant to, somehow, and we didn't know how to get back.

Leofric skidded to a halt in front of us. His eyes were shining, and he was flushed and panting.

'God in heaven, that's good fun,' he said.

'Joss says lots of people ride bikes in Gipeswic,' Merwenna told him, 'even girls. Imagine.'

'I know. It must be an amazing place,' Leofric said.

☙❧

CHAPTER SEVEN

∾

eldpruma
thunder fire (literal translation)

BATTLE

∾

The three of us were sitting under a clump of trees – walnut trees, Merwenna said – and I was tracing letters in the dirt with a stick.

'MERWENNA. That's how you write your name. I mean, that's how I would write it if I was back home. If I was in Gipeswic. And this is my name.'

I traced out JOSS.

Merwenna looked at me like I'd just split the atom.

'So…those marks, they mean our names?'

'Yeah. You can write anything, once you know what mark makes which sound. It's easy,' I said.

I didn't mean it was easy, exactly, only that I couldn't

imagine not being able to do it. Merwenna still looked awed.

'You're the first person I've known who can write. It's amazing, Joss...only the monks can read properly. Even Aesc can only read a little.'

I basked in her admiration like it was a warm bath. Lying next to us on the grass, Leofric, uninterested in the spelling lesson, twitched like a dog in his sleep.

My phone had been useless since I fell down the quarry, but I judged it to be about 9pm. It was a beautiful evening, warm and soft and loud with bees. The sky was pink and violet, and the first stars were beginning to appear in the violet parts. The air was very still; I took in deep breaths of it like someone taking great gulps of water.

Merwenna was practising tracing out her name in the dust when the sound of my own name being spoken nearby pricked me like a pin and got me listening.

The voices were coming from behind a thick tangle of hedge. It was Aesc, I thought, Aesc and somebody else.

'They're coming all right.' said the voice. 'The message Joss brought is the truth. I know you didn't believe him, but he was speaking the truth.'

I glanced at Merwenna, but she was still frowning and drawing patterns in the dust and I didn't think she had even noticed.

'They're ready to attack. Or almost ready.' the voice said. 'They're massing at Thetford with horses and men, and when they're ready, they'll be going for our throats.'

It was definitely Aesc. I put my hand on Merwenna's

wrist and put my finger up to my lips in a shh gesture.

'They sued for peace before,' another voice said, 'so they might do that again. Anyway, we were ready for them then, and we'll be ready this time as well.'

Merwenna had looked up by now. Her face was a mask of wondering.

I pressed my fingers to her lips.

Shh.

'We were *not* ready,' we heard Aesc say – icily, furious. 'We weren't ready then and we're not now. Four years ago, we bought them off, that's all. And getting them to agree to go nearly bankrupted the kingdom. We can't do that again.'

'It's my father...'

'I know. Shh.'

'Well, we'll defend our land,' I heard the other voice say. 'It's our land and they can't just walk in and take it from us by force. Not without a fight. We'll defend it to the last drop of blood of the last woman and the last witless child.'

It was Wuffa, I realised. I couldn't see him through the thick, green leafy hedge, but I knew it was him. He and Aesc must have walked here to talk in peace outside the village where no one could hear them.

'And what good would that be? When the blood of the last women and children is all over the ground, the Norsemen will be victorious, and the bloodshed won't have made the smallest difference.'

'We have to fight. Even if we lose, even if we know we're going to lose, we have to fight. What's the alternative? Lie down, say "help yourself"? We have to fight, there isn't a choice. We didn't start it, but we've got to finish it. We have to fight.'

There was a heavy noise, as if they'd both sat down on a log or something.

'The Norsemen are hungry for land,' Aesc said quietly, 'but that doesn't necessarily make them into demons. We were just the same all those generations ago. Maybe we can reason with them.'

I heard a noise which sounded like Wuffa was spitting on the ground.

'Reason with them… Are you insane? You can't reason with the Norsemen. You might as well say you want to talk a wolf out of taking your sheep.'

I heard Aesc sigh.

'You may well be right, Wuffa. Anyway, I doubt very much we'll get the chance to do much reasoning with them.' Merwenna had gone very still beside me. I saw her hand stretch out and grip Leofric's arm.

'We'll need to prepare,' Wuffa said.

'Yes. They won't be bought off this time. I don't want to fight, but I think we're going to have to.'

The log, or whatever it was they were sitting on, creaked as the two of them stood up to go.

We could hear their footsteps going off down the path, and then nothing.

I peered through the hedge.

'They've gone.'

Leofric yawned and stretched, and propped himself up on his elbow.

'What's the matter?' he asked.

I saw Merwenna swallow. Under her summer tan, her face was very pale.

'It was my father and Wuffa. They didn't know we were here. They were talking about the Norsemen.'

She stood up and smoothed the grass and bits of twigs off the front of her dress.

'They're getting ready to attack us again. I knew they'd come back one day,' she said.

Leofric scrambled up, scuffing the marks on the ground spelling out our names, and stood next to her. He put his hands on her shoulders and stared at her in a way that made me feel hot and awkward and in the way.

'I will not let anything bad happen to you,' he said. 'Do you hear me? I will not.'

Haegelisdun changed after that evening.

The fires in the forge were burning all day and all night, and wherever you went, you could hear the clanging of metal being hammered. Making new weapons, I thought, or sharpening up old ones. The perimeter fence was being raised and strengthened, and the hammering from this was blunter and higher but no less loud. And every day more men arrived: groups of toughs carrying axes and round shields, and richly dressed thanes on horseback. They were squeezed into the huts like the Tube in rush hour, but even so Haegelisdun soon ran out of places for them to sleep and they were slumped in the doorways and against the walls like heavily armed vagrants. During the day, they spent a lot of time in the fields above the village fighting one another; sometimes in individual hand-to-hand combat, and sometimes in the broad, sweeping moves of one group against another.

Training.

There was an air of menace that got to everyone. Even Osthryd wasn't giggling and patting and blushing any more.

Her big, ugly face turned up to me was emptied of all expression apart from fear. I liked it much better than the simpering smiles.

'Aren't you scared?' she asked.

The funny thing was, I wasn't. I couldn't seem to make myself understand that there would shortly be a real battle, with weapons and wounds and violence. *Battle*: even the word sounded childish and twangy and not-quite-real, more to do with dressing up and games of soldiers than real bloodshed.

'No I'm not, and you shouldn't be either. It'll be all right,' I said.

I put my hand on hers, and her skin was cold and sweaty the way it is when you are frightened.

'Last time they came, they didn't get as far as Haegelisdun,' she said. 'Aesc and King Edmund went to meet them and gave them so much money they agreed to go away. They went up North, I think, and laid waste to the cities up there.'

She crossed herself when she said King Edmund, and bobbed down like he was actually here, and she was bowing down before him.

'But they won't go away this time. They're coming to kill us.'

'Osthryd, they're not going to kill you,' I said. I wanted to say that things like that didn't happen, but it wouldn't have been true. I just wanted to say it, to make her feel better.

I tucked my arm through hers, and we went to down to the wood to collect kindling. No one worked in the dyeing sheds at the moment; everyone was busy getting ready for the assault, and there was no room and no time for anything else.

I wasn't afraid, exactly, but the air of tension made it impossible to relax. I ate supper with Cyneburga and the fourteen men who were sleeping on her floor, and then I said I was going out.

'Always wanting to be somewhere else. Can't sit still, not even for a minute,' Cyneburga said.

She wanted me to sit all evening and stare at the fire with her, the way Tracy used to want me to stare at the TV. But I thought I might explode unless I went out of the house.

It was a soft, powdery blue evening. I went out through the main gate – the only gate now, because Penda and some of the others had spent all day sealing up the other entrances – and walked quickly away from the village, until I couldn't hear the roar of the fires and the blacksmith's endless hammering any more. Instead, it was the shouts and clangs from what I was calling in my mind the practice pitch, but they sounded faint and far away.

I stood aside to let a herd of cows pass on their way home, and then I noticed a small figure walking towards me.

Merwenna, her walk already unmistakeable.

I caught up with her under the dappled shade of some trees. She was carrying a pitcher in each hand. I guessed she'd been taking water to the warriors on the practice pitch.

'Been giving out the half-time oranges?' I said.

Merwenna swapped the pitchers from hand to hand.

'You talk in riddles all the time, Joss. I can't understand half of what you say.'

'I'm sorry,' I said.

I took the empty jugs off her.

The singing of the birds was suddenly loud. But the shouts and noise from the practice field seemed even more far away and dreamy.

She stopped walking and took a deep breath.

'Joss. I feel…strange. I feel like all this, my whole life, is going to just end. I don't want it to. No one asked me. I didn't do anything to make it happen. But it's going to end, and there's nothing else.'

She looked up at me. The scattered freckles on her nose and forehead made me think of a sky full of stars.

'It could end at any moment, and what am I doing? Carrying on with stupid, normal things like fetching water and making bread. Like everything's the same but all the time, there's this awful thing that could happen any second.'

She was so pretty, it hurt. I felt something shift inside me, a painful tenderness that I didn't know how to deal with.

'I know. Like living on the slopes of a volcano,' I said.

'I don't know what that means!' she said. 'I want to understand, but I don't. I'm going to die not understanding anything you say to me.'

She covered her eyes with her hands.

'Oh, God, Merwenna. Don't cry,' I said.

I dropped the jugs onto the grass and wrapped my arms around her. She leant against me, her face pressed into my chest. My arms fitted around her perfectly. The scarf thing she usually wore over her hair had slipped down around her neck, and I could smell the outdoorsy, animal scent of her hair.

'It's all right, Merwenna. Don't cry. It's all right,' I said.

I couldn't get over it, the feel of her in my arms was so big and overwhelming it made me dizzy.

'It's all right.'

It was the only phrase that formed itself in my brain. *It's all right:* like a candle in the middle of the night; it might make a tiny glow of light in the bit of the darkness where you are, but it doesn't mean the night's not there, huge and black and threatening, just out of reach.

I squeezed her hand.

'Leofric will look after you. Aesc will look after you. They won't let anyone get near you,' I said.

Her hands were thin and light, the bones like twigs. My

arms were beginning to ache, but I wasn't going to be the first one to move. I would have stood there for all eternity if she'd wanted me to. I wouldn't have moved away if hordes of Vikings were descending on us from behind the trees. I realised that I'd imagined holding Merwenna in my arms so often, lying awake on the wooden bed listening to Cyneburga's snores, that to find it actually happening was difficult to believe.

Under my hands, I felt her shoulders straighten. She lifted her head up.

'I'm sorry, Joss.' she said.

There were the marks of tears on her face, but her eyes were calm, and she was smiling: a stiff, fake smile.

'Just a weak moment. We all have them.'

I picked up the water pitchers, and she held out her hands for them.

'I'll carry them. Thank you, Joss.'

'No, honestly. Let me stay with you,' I said.

'No, I'm fine now, truly. I'm going back, and I'd rather be on my own. You carry on with your walk.'

I brushed invisible bits of grass from my leggings.

'If you're sure,' I said.

She flashed the bright, meaningless smile at me again, and walked quickly and without looking back down towards Haegelisdun.

After she'd gone, I got that feeling you get when someone's watching you, and a little bit further on I saw that someone was.

It was Wuffa.

He was squatting against a young oak tree, and examining the blade of his sword, as if for flaws. As I got closer, he stuck the weapon back in its holder, and stepped onto the path, barring my way.

'I saw you with your hands all over Merwenna,' he said, 'God in heaven! You really are a piece of shit, aren't you? You know she's betrothed to Leofric, don't you?'

I ought to have been afraid, but just like with the imminent attack, somehow I wasn't. I was filled with a curious sense of detachment instead, like this was something I was watching on the television. At the same time, I knew Wuffa was right. He was only saying what was true, roughly and simply, the way he said everything, and the knowledge he was only speaking the truth made me defensive.

'Why don't you mind your own business?' I said.

I tried to go round him, but he edged his body in the way to stop me.

'You've betrayed Leofric,' he said. 'I should cut your arms off for this.'

I had been Tracy's son for sixteen years. I recognised empty, futile threats when I heard them.

'Fuck off, Wuffa,' I said.

I didn't feel brave, like I was standing up to him, but I just didn't care what he did or said. Even though I knew he was right. I'm not proud of it, but at that moment I couldn't have bothered less about what Wuffa or anyone else thought of me. The trees were so green they hurt my eyes, the birdsong so loud it hurt my ears; I had held

Merwenna in my arms close enough to feel her heartbeat under her skin, and the world was a beautiful place even if it was as dangerous as sitting on the slopes of a volcano.

℘℘

The next time I saw Leofric, it was clear that Wuffa couldn't have said anything to him about me and Merwenna, because he was his usual self: friendly and relaxed even in the teeth of a threatened invasion.

'Joss. Are you awake?' he hissed through the glassless window (wind-eye, Cyneburga called it).

'What time is it?' I whispered back.

It was dark in the house; I could just make out the humped block of Cyneburga in the bed on the other side of the room, and the floor black and lumpy with sleeping warriors.

'About an hour before dawn. I'm going up the hill to watch for invaders. Come on. I'll go and get your bike,' Leofric said.

I got up and dressed, and gave my hair a half-hearted drag through with Leofric's comb. I was getting used to not washing now, and didn't mind the interesting, sweaty smell of the clothes I wore. Toothpaste was a different thing – I couldn't get used to not having that. Scratching with twigs and rubbing with chalk wasn't the same, and judging by the state of the teeth of most people in Haegelisdun, it didn't work either.

Outside, the sky was inky colours, perfectly black in

parts, deep blue in others. There was a line of pink at the horizon. And the air was so fresh it was nearly painful in my lungs.

Balanced on Tim's bike, we freewheeled down to the river, pedalled along the path and then got off and climbed the hill, pushing the bike between us.

'Here,' Leofric said. 'You can see the whole valley from here, pretty much.'

I chucked the bike into a bush and came to stand beside him.

Haegelisdun lay below us, grey and shadowy in the half light, like we were looking at it through a fog. And the valley bottom, with the river beginning to glint as the sun came up, stretched away in front of us. Leofric was right; once the sun came up, we'd be able to see for miles.

He lay on his front and propped his chin up with his hands. The light grew paler and pinker every minute, until I could see him quite clearly, scanning the countryside from side to side like a searchlight, calm and absorbed in what he was doing. He was whistling through his teeth. There was a bitter taste in my mouth, and I spat to get rid of it.

I was jealous, that was my trouble. Leofric, blond and cheerful and self-possessed; the complete opposite of me. Leofric would never kick his heels, bored and cold, around a bleak Ipswich town centre on a rainy Saturday teatime, wondering what there was to do that evening, or what Tracy's next crisis might turn out to be, or how the rest of his life was going to pan out. He knew that already. His world might be an uncomfortable, mud-coloured place, with gritty food and lice in his hair and pits for toilets, the threat of violence always there, but it was his world and he was perfectly content with it, and perfectly sure of his place in it.

I was so jealous I could feel my skin prickle.

I forced myself to speak normally.

'I'm going to piss. Back in a minute.'

Leofric hadn't noticed my mood, or the tight way I was having to force the words out.

'Don't be long. I can't look down both sides of the valley at once,' he said.

I went into the bushes and kept going, past the bike, deeper and deeper. I walked quickly, getting out of breath, and soon I was wet all over with the dew. When I had walked for about ten minutes or so, I felt a bit calmer. I stopped, pissed, and headed back, and that was when I heard the noise: shouts and the clash of metal and the scuffle of men fighting.

Oh, God. It's happened. It's the Vikings.

I heard my name, desperately shouted in the tangle of all that noise. I forced my way through the brambles, but I was moving horribly, unbearably slowly. It was like one of those dreams where your legs don't work properly, and it feels like you're walking through quicksand.

I came out of the bushes and saw Leofric and three other men fighting on the riverbank. Leofric was still on his feet, but he was staggering against the three of them. If he fell, that'd be the end of it. They'd hack him to bits.

But they weren't Vikings. They were from some rival settlement miles away on the other side of the river, and it was simple bad luck that they'd found him here, alone and undefended. I'd worked it out: the people of Haegelisdun and from various other places hated each other, just like back home. If you're from Grange Wood, you hate anyone from Whitehorse. There's no reason for it, but you do. It's just the way things are.

I wanted to shout to Leofric to hold on, that I was coming, but my throat wasn't functioning either.

Which was a good thing, as it turned out.

I came out of the undergrowth on the slope about six metres above them, and right where I'd left my bike.

Mr Finch: use the element of surprise. They can't plan for that.

Mr Finch was right.

I got up to speed on the downward incline, so by the time I reached them I was going fast, fast enough to knock one of them right over with a kick of my foot.

'Leofric, jump on!'

It was a good thing he'd practised so much on my bike because it couldn't have been easy, jumping onto a moving crossbar when two ugly men are trying to knock out your brains with long-handled swords. There was a cut on his cheek you could have posted a letter in.

He was still slashing at them with his sword arm as the overloaded bike careened down the bumpy path.

'For God's sake, Leofric,' I panted, 'I'm trying to *balance*.'

We were on the flat by now, and it was far more difficult

to go quickly. I was standing up on the pedals to get more speed from the bike, and the whole thing was lurching violently and alarmingly from side to side.

'Mind the branch!'

It was Leofric's voice, and yet it wasn't a normal voice; it seemed to be going round and round in circles, echoing with reverb: mind the *branch* mind the *branch* mind the *branch*. It made me dizzy.

I saw a bright flash of light blue sky, stamped with a black design of leaves. There was plenty of time to notice it because everything seemed to happen in slow motion. Then there was a crack like a firework exploding, and a small starburst that blinded me for a second. And Leofric's voice, mind the *branch* mind the *branch*, although this was getting fainter and further away.

And then there was a pain in my head so enormous I couldn't think about anything else.

CHAPTER EIGHT

❧

haukbroðs
hawk table (literal translation)

ARM

❧

The sound of voices: several voices mingling together so I couldn't hear the words. A flashing, greenish light that got into my eyes and annoyed me.

TrytokeepstillformeJoss.

It was a woman's voice. The words separated themselves out, and the voice was one of those calm, soothing ones.

'Try to keep still for me, Joss.'

I felt someone pulling at my sleeve, then smooth, cool fingers on my arm.

'Small scratch on your arm coming up.'

A man's voice, this time.

'I'm just going to pop a stiff collar around your neck,' he said. 'Can you hear me, Joss? Can you open your eyes for me?'

I tried, but the bright, annoying flashing meant I screwed them almost shut again immediately.

Looming above me, in the space between the flashes, there had been a face I almost recognised.

A thin, worried face wearing glasses. A beard so bushy a family of animals could nest there.

My mind formed the word: Tim.

I felt my bones jolt against each other as I was lifted up.

'Lie still old son,' a voice said to me, and so I did. I lay very, very still, as if by not moving I could work out just what the hell was happening now.

'You'll be all right Joss,' Tim said, 'you'll be fine. We're just going to the hospital as a precaution. To make sure you haven't done any damage falling twenty feet into the quarry.'

Metal doors shut off the flashing greenish light, and a siren began urgently wailing.

'Is this an ambulance?' I said.

The woman with the calm voice said, 'Don't worry, Joss. It won't take long, and John's a good driver. He'll try not to jolt you too much.'

She had short, dark hair, and a kind smile. Her breath smelt of mint. She leant over me and strapped me to the stretcher thing I was lying on. Tim was sitting on the other side, on a little folding seat, and she helped him with his seatbelt, which he was fumbling with like he'd never seen one before.

He stretched over and took my hand. Which sounds cringey, but I found I didn't mind it, except it made my eyes fill with tears so that I had to blink hard.

What was going on? How could something as real as Haegelisdun, with its noisy animals and Saturday-night drinking songs about battles and valour; its mud and smell from the toilet pits, and gritty food that stuck in your teeth; how could all that simply vanish? It had been real. I'd believed Haegelisdun existed like I believed Australia existed: a real place where real people lived real lives. Last week, I'd taught Leofric and his friends to play football; we'd had a sack packed full of straw for a ball, and the score had been 15–12, and I remembered it like it was yesterday, because it almost was.

The shock of finding all this gone left me feeling winded. The ambulance woman tucked a red blanket around me, but it wasn't cold that was making my teeth chatter, it was shock.

I kept on keeping still. And I said nothing; I was afraid that if I opened my mouth all that would come out would be stammering about Merwenna and Haegelisdun, and incoherent questions that made no sense. I didn't want them to think that I was mad. But I was afraid – I was really afraid – that I might be.

Tim started to talk to me, telling me how he and Cressida had got worried when it grew dark and I wasn't home, and even more worried when I didn't answer my phone.

'We took a car each and just drove around looking,' he

said. 'It took me half an hour to find you. I've told Cressida you're all right. She'll meet us at the hospital and take us home.'

He kept squeezing and patting my hand like he didn't know what to do with it, but didn't want to stop touching me.

'Half an hour...oh, God.'

Talking made the pain in my head worse. It felt like someone was pushing needles into the space behind my eyes.

Half an hour.

But I'd been in Haegelisdun for weeks. We'd got most of the harvest in.

I was mad. There was no other explanation. I had imagined the whole thing, like I'd told myself at the beginning; it had been my brain buzzing out of control following a crack on the head. But the thing was, I hadn't really believed it – certainly not after the second day. How could it not be real? I could remember perfectly the texture of the grass and the harsh coats of the dogs. And the stink of their breath. I remembered laughing like a drain at Leofric's jokes. I remembered exactly how it felt to hold Merwenna in my arms.

But here I was in the ambulance. So I had to be going mad, there was no other explanation, and this frightened me so much I began to shake again.

Then I remembered something. I remembered that, when I'd come back from pissing in the bushes, I'd felt the lump of Leofric's comb in the pocket of my tunic.

Which meant it had to be there now, since it was only a few minutes ago.

'Try not to wriggle, Joss,' the ambulance woman said.

'Just trying to get something,' I said.

I squirmed my hands down underneath the tight red blanket, feeling for the pocket, and then I got another shock.

I'd been wearing Eadwig's tunic and peculiar baggy leggings. But now I could feel I was back in Tim's Lycra bike stuff. It encased me like a thick and sweaty layer of extra skin. I recognised the feel of it even without being able to see it.

'My comb...I can't find it,' I said.

The ambulance was noisy and rattly inside, and that demented siren outside made it hard to hear properly.

'Don't worry about your phone now. We've found you, that's the main thing.'

'Comb, not phone...oh shit,' I said, 'it must have fallen out of my pocket when we were at the lookout place. Or on the bike.'

I felt, rather than saw, the two of them exchange a quick, sympathetic glance. They thought I was raving. Maybe I was. I slumped back on the pillow and closed my eyes. The stiff collar pinched into my neck.

'Don't worry about the bike, Joss,' Tim said, 'we'll find it. And anyway, it doesn't matter if we don't – things don't matter. People are what matters.'

So it was the A and E department of the Norfolk and Norwich hospital, and three hours in a cubicle with a torn curtain and walls painted a hard, shiny grey. They made me get undressed and wear one of those gowns that are supposed to do up at the back. They X-rayed me and gave me painkillers when I said my head ached.

'Your dad can stay with you,' the nurse said as she checked – for something like the tenth time – the name band they'd fastened round my wrist. 'It might be a little while before the doctor comes. We're a bit busy this evening.'

It made me laugh to think of Tim being anyone's dad, let alone mine. But I was touched by his staying with me. The noise and sense of urgent rushing coming from behind the torn curtain made us not want to say anything somehow, and so we sat more or less in silence, but it was still good to feel him there. The painkillers started to work, and I think I may have gone to sleep for a while.

And then the torn curtains opened and a sleek, Asian guy in a white coat came in.

'I'm Dr Khoo,' he said, 'and you're a very lucky young man. No bones broken, no concussion to speak of. Just superficial bruising.'

Something about his tone, and the way he was looking at me, suggested he thought I should thank him personally.

I didn't say anything. I was so afraid I was going insane that I didn't want to speak in case they guessed. I'd had to go and see Tracy in Woodlawns in Ipswich a few times, and it had been enough to know I never wanted to go anywhere like that again.

'You can get off home,' Dr Khoo said breezily. 'Don't go falling into any more quarries.'

Suddenly, I remembered something.

'Just a minute. What about this?' I asked.

I pulled back the sleeve of the hospital gown and showed him my left arm. The cut made by Wuffa's sword was maybe twenty centimetres long, fat in the middle and tapering to thinner at the edges. Along its outer edges, it was swollen and shiny and pale red in colour. It didn't hurt any more, but it was quite impressive-looking.

Dr Khoo looked taken aback at the sight of it.

'When did you do this?'

'When I fell into the quarry. It wasn't there this morning, was it Tim?'

He looked closely at my arm and then at me.

'But this tissue is granulating! This wound is weeks old. You ought to have had it stitched, but it's too late now.'

I could feel a smile stretching itself over my face, I couldn't help it.

'Weeks old, yeah?'

He gave me a suspicious look.

'At least. Listen, Joss. Did you do this? Did you hurt yourself on purpose?'

I caught a glimpse of it again: contempt disguised as concern.

'No. It was someone else.'

I pulled the gown off over my head and plucked Tim's damp, sweaty Lycra cycling top from the heap at the bottom of the trolley.

'Let's go home, Tim.'

I watched him fumbling with the buttons on his blocky old mobile phone, calling Cressida to come and get us. Dr Khoo was still watching me like he suspected me of something, but I was too happy to care.

I hadn't imagined it. I wasn't mad. And Merwenna was real, as real as the granulating, weeks-old wound made by Wuffa on my arm.

'Home' had slipped out without my meaning it to.

'Fixed-term exclusion. Yeah, I thought that might happen,' I said.

Consequences, Ms Osborne had said, and I'd known what she meant.

Cressida pushed the letter to me across the kitchen table.

'Sit down. I'll get you some tea. Read the letter, and we'll decide what we're going to do.'

I skimmed through it.

'There's nothing we *can* do, is there?'

Cressida poured tea. 'I don't know. There might be. They're supposed to try other things first; a fixed-term exclusion's supposed to be the last option, not the first.'

I wondered how she knew all this stuff. Maybe she used to be a teacher. Or a parent, although there weren't any photos plastered all over the place of kids or grandchildren, like in the homes of people with a family.

Maybe she just knew stuff.

I pointed at a bit in the letter.

'Yeah, but look. They say "serious violent and threatening behaviour". That's why they've gone straight for the nuclear option. Because I was so serious and threatening and violent.'

Cressida regarded me steadily over the rim of her teacup.

'We can protest, if you want. We can object to it. I'll find the school's behaviour policy, and see if we can find something they've done wrong or not done. There usually is. Do you want to?'

I blinked a few times and drank some tea so she couldn't see my face.

'No, forget it. Nothing we do'll make a difference. Let them do what they like,' I said.

I told myself I didn't care, and in a way it was true.

'But thanks,' I added.

The letter ended by inviting – it actually said that, *inviting* – Cressida and Tim and me to the meeting Ms Osborne had talked about on the phone. To Discuss the Situation.

☺☺

Ms Osborne began by saying there was nothing to discuss.

'We don't have any choice but to exclude you, Joseph. Physical violence will never, never be tolerated in any school in Suffolk.'

Her voice and tone and every muscle of her face was

grave and serious, but there was a stagey quality to the seriousness, like she'd practised it in front of a mirror.

'You make it sound like it was bloody hand-to-hand combat, like we were fighting to the death or something. It was a scrap in the boys' toilets, that's all,' I said, 'and he started it. Rufus Whatshisname.'

The man sitting next to Ms Osborne, a suit from the local education authority, leant forward. He'd told us his name at the beginning but I'd forgotten it.

'You'll have your opportunity to speak at the end, Joseph,' he said.

Sofia used to say things like that all the time, which was how I knew it wasn't true.

'You weren't there,' I said, 'so you don't know what happened. There were four of them and one of me, and they started it. What about *their* physical violence? They were going to stick my bloody head down the toilet. Is Rufus Palmier-Whatever going to be excluded as well?'

The suit said he wasn't going to discuss the details of other students' cases, and the conversation sickened and died.

I glared at him. He was wearing an expression every bit as concerned and serious as Ms Osborne, but just like hers, there was something phoney about it. I mean, what did he care?

'You're an intelligent boy, Joss,' he said. 'Don't turn your back on the opportunities education can offer you.'

The phrase sounded lumpy and false when he said it, like it was a slogan rather than anything anyone would actually say, and I didn't bother to reply. I nearly did – I had quite a lot to say about Opportunities as they applied to people like me and Tracy and the twins, but in the end, I said nothing. There was no point.

Cressida stood up.

'Give a dog a bad name and hang him. That's not even *allowed* in English law. If that's all, I think we'll go home,' she said. She shook hands with Ms Osborne, and with the suit from the LEA. I didn't think they'd expected her to – I think they expected her to flounce out and slam the door.

I hadn't heard the expression before, the one about the dog, but I knew what she meant, and she was right.

So I had four days off while my cuts and bruises healed, and it was hotter than ever and I was missing Merwenna and Tracy and Alice and Ipswich and Haegelisdun so much that I felt permanently annoyed and anxious, the way you feel when you're looking for something and can't remember where you put it. It was too hot outside, but indoors the rooms were all dark and cluttered with stuff that wasn't mine, and so cool you felt you were at the bottom of a well.

'Come outside. You can help me pick the raspberries,' Cressida said.

'Sofia's coming,' I said. There'd been a phone call first thing: the school would have told her about the exclusion and so she was on her way, as eager to probe and discuss and blame as a scent hound after a rabbit.

'I know. But not till lunchtime. We'll do gardening till she arrives. It'll put us in a good mood,' Cressida said.

'Oh, all right,' I said. I didn't want to move, but once I got outside, I felt better than I had indoors and anyway I quite liked picking raspberries, pushing back the furry leaves and finding them there, like soft, hidden jewels.

'They're early this year. It's the heat,' Cressida said.

Her face floated into view between the thick, green leaves and the raspberry canes. She was wearing a white straw hat, tied under her chin with a scarf. She looked very peculiar.

'Because of global warming, you mean?' I asked.

I felt like I knew quite a lot about global warming because Tracy used to worry about it a lot. I think it was because it used to take her mind off worrying about other stuff like how the hell she was going to pay the council tax. Or because she muddled the world's problems up with her own, so that in her head everything was a tangle of helplessness and hopelessness. Opportunities, hah!

'No, it's just a hot summer, that's all. Global warming…I don't know. The world's had Ice Ages, and before them England was a tropical rainforest. And Dickens used to write about the Thames freezing over and people skating on it. Things go in cycles, don't they? Everything comes back again, like a pendulum.'

Sometimes when Cressida and Tim said things, I was conscious of a vast store of knowledge, things I had no idea about, just out of my reach. Like a library full of books behind a closed door.

I said, 'Dickens?'

Her face bobbed out again from behind the leaves.

'Charles Dickens. I'll lend you one of his books if you like. Now you've got four days off school, it ought to be long enough to polish off *David Copperfield*.'

Sofia came after lunch. She kept a still, disappointed look on her face during the whole hour she sat at the kitchen table, saying over and over how she didn't want to be drawn into a discussion about the rights and wrongs of what happened at Easterbrook. Which made two of us. She kept waving this Behaviour Contract about, insisting I sign it; there was a section for Cressida and Tim to sign as well to confirm they would support my efforts to improve my behaviour.

When we'd all signed on the dotted lines, Cressida was polite and offered tea. I propped my face up on my hands and stared at Sofia. I liked doing this because it clearly drove her mad and made her nervous as hell, judging from the restless movements of her hands. I thought she would probably break into speech any moment and I was right. Her sort can't bear silence for longer than a second or two. It unsettles them.

'Not a very good start at Easterbrook, Joss, was it?' she said.

I carried on staring at her.

Tim came in with a tray of tea. He gave me a fleeting ghost of a smile across the kitchen table as if he could tell how much Sofia was getting on my nerves. I nodded at him. I noticed idly, the way you notice things that aren't important, that he had little specks of brown sugar in his beard.

And then I noticed something else.

Sofia was talking, on and on; I had faded out the noise she made so that it was no more intrusive that a fly buzzing against a high window somewhere.

Which is when it banged into my mind – I hadn't even been thinking about Haegelisdun – that Tim could have been Aesc's twin brother.

It was the beard that had hidden it till now, but take that away, and the glasses, and you could see it more clearly: the fine, friendly lines around the tired eyes, the worried, twisty smile and gappy front teeth. The gentle way he had of speaking and moving.

I was so staggered by this that I had to go and sit in the downstairs loo and take some deep, steadying breaths.

So that was it. I had imagined the whole thing. Wuffa and Merwenna and Leofric and Aesc: all nothing more than flickers from an injured brain.

I dragged my hand across my face. The awful truth of it hit me: I was mad after all.

CHAPTER NINE

❧❧

heofon-candel
heaven candle (literal translation)

SUN

❧❧

I didn't know how long I'd been there when I became aware that someone had been knocking on the door.

'Are you all right in there?'

It was Cressida; I must have been sitting there for ages, fully clothed on the edge of the toilet seat.

'I'm fine. Don't fuss,' I said.

'Sofia's going back in a minute,' Cressida said through the door. 'You should come out, say goodbye to her.'

'Yeah. All right. In a minute,' I said.

I heard her going away, and then my arm started to hurt and when I pulled back my sleeve, there it was. The most beautiful sight in the world.

The wound from Wuffa gleamed across my forearm: pink and white and shiny, a pink worm against the dark of my skin; thickly ridged when I trailed my fingers across it. Relief washed over me like a wave breaking over a rock.

I didn't understand it, but I told myself I didn't have to. And after another minute or so, my heart stopped hammering so hard, and I took a deep breath and unlocked the door.

I went into the study because I could still hear Sofia chirping away in the kitchen and I couldn't face it yet. And I needed another minute to get myself geared up for the sight of Tim drinking his tea, looking like Aesc and talking with Aesc's voice.

But then Tim came into the study to find me.

He said, 'Joss. What are you doing here? Are you looking for a book?'

'*David Copperfield*,' I said, although actually I'd been gazing at the rows of colourful spines without even seeing them.

'Oh. Well, never mind that now. We've got at least three copies, I'll find one for you. But you've got a visitor in the kitchen.'

'She's not my visitor…' I began.

'I didn't mean Sofia. It's a girl from school. Her name's Alice,' Tim said.

Alice. At the sound of her name, my heart started its mad hammering again. But I was annoyed as well, annoyed with her for coming round like that, just turning up and assuming I wouldn't mind. It was like she'd tried to catch me off-guard. Because school was one thing, but now I was unprepared for her; I felt foolish and exposed and at a horrible disadvantage, like she'd caught me watching children's TV or picking stuff out of my teeth.

I was almost angry with her. I didn't realise how angry till I came into the dim, untidy kitchen and saw her standing there, gleaming with health and that perfect, moisturised skin, glowing next to Cressida, who looked like a crumpled dog's dinner. Suddenly, I was furious. She'd come round because she knew I was in trouble. A knight in shining bloody armour, to rescue me. It annoyed the hell out of me, but at the same time there was a glad, leaping feeling inside me at the sight of her.

This made me furious as well.

'Hello, Joss,' she said.

A picture flicked into my mind of Merwenna: the skinny wrists, her hands covered in scratches from all the stuff she did all day, every day. Alice, smiling, a flash of perfect teeth, hardly seemed real beside it. She was like a doll, an expensive, smiling doll.

'Alice just came to see if you're all right,' Cressida said.

I bet she did.

I was conscious of Sofia, watching us like a cat watches a mouse hole.

Act normal.

'Yeah, right. Thank you, Alice. I've been suspended for a week, thanks to lovely Ms Osborne.'

'I know. I heard,' she said.

She looked up at me through caterpillar lashes, let

her hair swing. I felt like shaking her, telling her I could see right through her. That I didn't need a saviour. But at the same time, the dazzle of her, her smile, made me desperately glad she had come.

'Sofia Bassett-Torres, Joss's social worker,' Sofia said, firmly.

Alice said, 'How do you do?' I hadn't known people actually said that.

'Come on, Alice. Let's go for a walk,' I said.

I couldn't wait to get her out of there, away from Cressida in her tatty, embarrassing skirt and tenderly wrinkled face; her knee socks and the battered old Crocs on her feet, and Tim's big bristly beard. I felt fiercely protective of them. Next to Alice, they looked like remnants from a human jumble sale.

'I'll see you next week, Joss. To review the contract,' Sofia said.

I took a deep breath, inhaling the scent of Alice: soap and clean clothes and flowery perfume. The smell of money. I took another breath, and managed not to tell Sofia what to do with her Acceptable Behaviour Contract.

We walked up the shadowy green lane into the village. I'd had a vague idea about taking her for a drink – there was a pub called the Crown on the edge of the green – but when I put my hand in my pocket I found I had hardly any money, not even enough for two Cokes. Also, I couldn't be bothered. The idea of sitting opposite her over a pub table, thinking of things to say to make her smile, seemed like just too much effort. I found that all I wanted to do was walk about outside with her; my bad temper was dissolving into nothing just having her next to me, not touching her or saying anything, just being side by side. The fierce heat of the day was giving way to something softer, and the shadows of the trees on the green had lengthened and crept almost as far as the old-fashioned red phone box on the corner.

It was nice of her to come, I realised. I suddenly understood that feeling protective about someone didn't automatically translate into looking down on them. I'd felt protective about Cressida, hadn't I? Maybe protective feelings were just one of the ways you loved someone. Maybe it didn't have to mean you thought they were a problem to be solved, or an interesting piece of rough.

'Tell me something,' I said.

We had got to the edge of the copse, and the green, woody smell of it was all around us.

'Tell me something, and answer me truthfully,' I said.

'Yes?'

'Truthfully, right?' I took a deep breath. 'Do you believe in time travel?'

She hadn't been expecting that. Probably she'd been expecting something gentle and sly, like how she felt about me. Something teenage and personal and cringey.

'Um...OK. Time travel,' she said. 'Yes, I suppose it must be...like that film, the one where monkeys rule the world instead of people. You know, if you go fast enough, you go faster than time and end up in the future. Einstein, the theory of relativity. You know.'

She frowned, trying to remember what film it had been. I liked her much more now we were out of Cressida's kitchen, and she'd abandoned the lashes thing. I liked her a lot, I realised, because she had answered the question properly, without pretending not to understand.

'What about the other way,' I said, 'going backwards, into the past?'

'Oh, God, ghosts,' she said, 'no, of course not... I don't believe in any of that stuff. Ghosts, going back in time. Why, do you?'

I hadn't quite meant ghosts; not exactly. But then again, I wasn't sure what I had meant.

I found her hand and gripped it, hard.

'I don't know,' I said.

She stared at me for a long moment, and then she laughed.

'Joss, you're so...I've never met anyone like you before,' she said.

'You don't know what I'm like; not really,' I said.

'No, but the bits I do know. They're interesting,' she said.

She moved a tiny bit closer. I looked back at her. There was a quietness and stillness about her that you don't get very often, and that was another thing that I liked about her. But I wasn't going to let her take a holiday in me. I wasn't going to let her use me as a piece of rough, even a little bit.

'I've never met anyone from your…you know. Background.'

'Might make things a bit difficult,' I said. Gentle and sly. We hadn't kissed yet, but we both knew we were going to.

'I don't see why. People's backgrounds aren't important. It's where you're going that matters, not where you come from,' Alice said.

I wanted to ask her if she got all her opinions from fridge magnets, or only that one. But the thing was, she believed it, and anyway, for someone like Alice it was true.

Her confidence touched me. I pulled her towards me and kissed her. I kissed her for a long time, and while I was doing it, I was telling myself I must always remember this: the first time I kissed Alice. But even though I was fiercely concentrating on how it felt, I had a strange, tangled feeling inside me that it wasn't just Alice in my arms but Merwenna as well. As if the two of them were one person, dissolved together so you couldn't tell them apart, like salt in water.

But when I opened my eyes, it was Alice standing there, leaning against me: golden, beautiful Alice, smiling and tasting of mouthwash like at the dentist's.

'Oh, Joss,' she said, 'is this a good idea, do you think? Us, I mean. I don't want anyone to get hurt.'

Us?

'Us,' I said, imitating her breathless voice. 'Oh, God, who knows? Anyway, you can't spend your whole life worrying about getting hurt. Getting hurt is part of being alive.'

I didn't expect her to believe this. I knew it was true, but why should she?

'Right,' she said. 'You're right, I think. We'll risk it. We'll risk getting hurt.'

She pressed closer to me. I found I was touched by her, more touched than I ever remembered being by anything. She snaked her arms around my back. In my arms, she was sleeker and more solid than Merwenna had been.

'Let's not go through the copse,' she said, 'let's stay out in the sun. That way's over the bridge anyway, and you know what I told you about that. It's bad luck to cross it.'

'Why? Are we getting married?'

Sometimes when Alice smiled, she looked like a sleepy cat.

'You never know,' she said, 'and I don't want to take any chances.'

Once my four days' exclusion was over, it was back to Easterbrook and the new experience of being with Alice. I didn't worry any more about being mad. I felt much better about it, because I didn't *feel* mad. And as the days passed, without me opening the doors to cupboards and finding myself in the Stone Age or at the court of King Arthur or something, it got harder and harder to believe anything had happened at all. If it hadn't been for the scar, I might have told myself to forget the whole thing.

Like they say in the old-fashioned story books Tracy

used to read to the twins, the days passed. And the weeks, and then it was almost a month since I moved to Hoxne, and then June turned into July and the summer term was almost over. Every time I caught sight of Alice in the corridors at school, the joy made my chest start tightening up. When she brushed her fingers accidentally across the back of my hand, like when I was holding a tray in the cafeteria or something, I could feel the little zings of electricity going right through me down to my feet.

But I wasn't her dirty little secret. The whole of Easterbrook knew about the two of us – our Relationship, as Alice liked to call it. I hated the word, hearing in it the sob and blub of stupid magazines or celebrities on TV, but if she wanted to say it, I wasn't going to stop her. I couldn't care less what she called it. I didn't even think it had to have a name. She paraded me like a torch, and I could feel the waves of hate coming off Rufus Palmier-Thompson every time I went anywhere near him.

'I've got something to ask you,' Alice said one day.

It was the lunch hour, and we were lying on the scorched, scratchy grass outside the science block. You could hear the calls and cries of the tennis players, and the 'pock' sounds of tennis balls from the courts behind us. It was so hot I could feel the sweat forming all over me. I would stick to the grass if I tried to sit up.

'Is it about time travel?' I asked, without opening my eyes.

'No, idiot. It's about lunch on Sunday. At mine. My mum and dad want to meet you.'

I said nothing. I didn't like the sound of it at all, but I knew when I didn't have a choice.

⊚⊚

'Of course you must go,' Cressida said. 'You've been asked. It would be rude not to go.'

She suggested taking some flowers from the garden, to give to Alice's mother, but I felt stupid enough without that.

Alice lived in one of the new houses I'd seen that first day from the bus stop.

When you got up close, the houses were enormous, and the gardens that surrounded them were spotless and new as if the lawns had been laid that morning. Expensive cars gleamed on every drive. And everywhere you looked, it was all immaculately clean, not a trace of litter or dirt or mess. You could eat your dinner off the dustbins.

Dinner: it was Sunday, so I was expecting meat and potatoes and gravy, only the table in the sun room – the first sun room I had ever been in – was laid with a giant china bowl of salad and dishes of olives and flat white discs of cheese, so I didn't think it could be.

Alice was glowing and excited, hanging on to my arm.

'Say hello to Joss, Mummy,' she said.

Mummy. Alice's mother was tall and thin and smiling, and when she said hello her voice was Alice's voice, only lower and crisper. She looked like her too, a faded version. A version of Alice that had been left too long in the sun room. Her bare, braceleted arms were lean and muscular. Tennis, I guessed. You could definitely picture her playing tennis.

'Please. Call me Vanessa,' she said.

Well, that was impossible, obviously.

Alice's father came into the sun room with a hand outstretched ready for me to shake, and a mouthful of gleaming teeth set in a curved smile. Perhaps he was a dentist.

'Joss, you're welcome. *More* than welcome,' he said.

It was awful. I liked it when it was just me and Alice, walking around Hoxne and sitting on stiles to talk. I liked finding an empty classroom at school or a quiet corner of the Easterbrook library, but this was awful. Their bright smiles, the friendly questions, it was all phoney as hell. They were pretending that it didn't matter to them one bit that I was a foster kid from an Ipswich housing estate, suspended from school in his first week, but I knew it was fake and so did they and I felt my hackles rising like dogs do when they know the other dogs don't like them.

'It's a shame Liberty can't be here,' Alice's father said.

He said it so seriously I thought he was making some kind of weird political statement. But it turned out that Liberty was Alice's older sister, away at university. I'd known she'd had one, just not what her ridiculous name was.

'She's doing history of art, at Jesus. Cambridge University,' he added, in the slow, kind tones of someone explaining things to an Aztec.

Every time I said anything, they turned polite, eager listening faces towards me, as if a foreigner was attempting English conversation.

And then Alice's mother – Vanessa – brought in a big, square pottery dish containing dinner, which was ribbons of pasta and flecks of green stuff in a slippery whitish sauce.

'Fettucine Alfredo. Lucky none of us need to diet,' she said, and Alice and her father laughed, as if she'd made some sort of a joke.

Without being invited to, I helped myself to salad. I'd intended to assert myself, grabbing hold of the wooden salad servers to show them I wasn't overawed by their white sofas and Fettucine Alfredo, but it backfired. They watched me pile green leaves onto my plate, then Vanessa quietly said perhaps they'd better toss the salad. She dripped oil from a little jug into the pottery bowl, and churned it all up with the wooden spoons. The silence while she did this was horrific.

I gave up then. I let them carry on with the gracious fake friendliness and smiles. I knew they were relieved that I was no worse, and also that they saw me as a temporary, unfortunate blip in their daughter's life, but one they were easily up to overpowering. It made me so furious that I found myself adopting a kind of cocky, charmless bravado that even I could see was repellent and ridiculous. I kept it up for the hours and hours and hours it took to eat the Lunch, letting my accent slip with my table manners, because there wasn't any point in trying, was there? Their

kind, understanding smiles grew wider and wider till they
filled the whole of the sun room with their victory.

👁👁

'What was all that about?' Alice asked.

I saw that her eyes had gone shiny with tears.

'What was all what about?'

We were at the bottom of the drive. The gleaming
bonnet of Alice's father's expensive car lay between us like
an impenetrable force field.

'Why are you so rude to everyone?'

I didn't answer. There probably was an answer, but I
didn't know it.

'My mum and dad went out of their way to be nice to
you.'

'Nice. Is that what you call it?'

She was properly crying now. I loved her, and I had
made her cry. I tried to reach over the car bonnet to touch
her, tried to say sorry, but the words wouldn't come, and
my hands stayed down, fists curled into balls, by my side.

'I don't know why you have to be so horrible. Do you
think we're terrible people? Do you hate us?'

'No, of course I…'

'What, then?'

She looked up at me with none of the eyelash batting.
Just sad blue eyes, drowning in tears.

I felt suddenly vicious. The softness that had crept into
me earlier, when Alice had come round that first time,

when I'd kissed her, had shattered like a plate dropped onto a hard floor. The tenderness I'd felt was wiped out, replaced by the old anger. I didn't see it – our *relationship* – as stemming from protectiveness any more.

'Smug. You're so smug. I don't know how it doesn't choke you.'

I heard her gasp, like I'd slapped her. I knew I was being unfair. More than unfair, but I was too miserable to care, or be anything else.

I walked out of the drive and quickly down the road. I didn't look back.

CHAPTER TEN

❦❦

ferðloca
box of spirits (literal translation)

BODY AND SOUL

❦❦

The Waveney Family Centre was a sad place, all peeling paint and those thick, gurgling radiators that are tepid all year round and make the air smell of dust. Someone had painted a Disney mural in the corridor leading to the family room, probably to cheer the place up a bit, but if that was the aim, it hadn't worked. In fact, it had the opposite effect. It wasn't very good, for one thing – Mickey and Goofy and the rest of them were distorted and out of proportion – and the bright, splodgy colours only made the original dinginess look worse. There were posters stuck on top of the Disney characters advising about needle exchange and that Benefit Fraud is a Crime.

'Are you sure you are all right, Joss?' Sofia asked gently, as if she expected me to break down in tears or something.

I said that I was. She held open the door to the family room, and I went inside.

Tracy looked different. She was sitting curled up in a chair by the window, and she looked smaller than I remembered. And she'd dyed her hair. The bright blonde I remembered, with the dark badger-tip roots, was gone and her hair was now orange: the brilliant, toxic orange of tinned tomato soup.

'Hello, Tracy,' I said.

'Joss,' Tracy said cautiously.

I'd been worried the twins wouldn't remember me, but they did. I crouched down on the floor and held out my arms, and the two of them toddled towards me as casually as if they'd seen me yesterday. I'd forgotten the small, solid packed weight of them, and the special smell of their heads.

'Joss. Titty, titty,' Virginia said.

I set her down. 'Is that the kind of language they've been teaching you at the Park?'

'No, she's trying to tell you about the kitty. The cat. Their foster parents have got a Siamese cat,' said Tracy.

'That's nice.'

'And Sylvia has two more teeth. Show Joss your teeth, Sylvia.'

Her skinny fingers were twitching in her lap; I could tell she was longing for a cigarette. I felt a rush of sympathy mixed with irritation.

She huddled in that chair, so defeated by it all that she

hardly seemed to notice Virginia and Sylvia. I knew she loved them – I knew she loved all three of us – but sitting there like a stunned bird that's flown into a window was a mistake. Sofia and the other woman from the Family Centre needed to see kisses and cuddles and tears. They were making notes, for God's sake.

'Play with the girls, Tracy,' I muttered.

'What? Oh, I can't, Joss, I'm tired out. I've not been sleeping properly. The doctor gave me some tablets but they don't work properly. I wake up every night at two in the morning.'

Her voice was a whine of tiredness and self-pity.

I was so full of helpless sadness and anger that for a moment I couldn't speak. Then I turned back to the twins, and their sea of crappy plastic toys from the Family Centre toy box.

'OK, girls. What shall we play with?' I asked.

'How are you feeling, Joss? It's good to hear you are getting on better at school,' Sofia said.

Her pen was poised to write it down: How I Was Feeling.

I didn't answer at first, partly because it was none of her business, but also because couldn't she guess how I was feeling? Angry, sad, lonely. I would have thought it was totally obvious.

'Oh. I'm all right,' I said. She bent her head and wrote something down in her notebook.

☺☺

Back at Easterbrook on Monday, I was still hung over with misery from the Family Centre and the lunch at Alice's.

Despite the disaster on Sunday, I felt the same about her; whatever it was called – and unlike Alice, I didn't need to have labels for everything – it hadn't changed. She was having nothing to do with me, quite rightly. But from Mr Richards' classroom you could see over the tennis courts, and if she was there playing, I could watch her and feel quite ill with longing.

The rest of the time, I just felt hollow and empty, as if there was nothing to look forward to ever again. No one had spoken to me much at Easterbrook apart from Alice, so now I was pretty much on my own. Which I didn't mind – God knows, I had nothing to say to anyone here – but you do miss the sound of your own voice when you've literally not said a word to anyone for hours.

'A penny for your thoughts.'

Oh, God. I looked up, irritated.

Mr Richards, class teacher and Anglo-Saxon expert, sat uninvited on my desk. It was lunchtime and blazing hot outside. The classroom had been empty when I'd come in, and that was how I preferred it.

'You looked lost in thought.'

His voice had a Welsh tang. He was as out of place in deepest rural Suffolk as I was.

I stared in front of me. He'd give up eventually and leave

me in peace.

'Well?' he said.

I shook my head.

'Lost in thought, and that's unusual. You don't usually find a student, or anyone really, just doing nothing. Just thinking. Usually they're twiddling away with their silly little phones or taking photos of each other, or texting silly messages...twiddle, twiddle, twiddle. It's as if their hands can't bear to be still.'

He watched me beadily. He was a small man with receding ginger hair, the kind of hair that looked as if it would be coarse and springy to touch, like heather.

'Do you have an answer?' he said.

'An answer, what for?'

'There, now,' he said triumphantly, 'I knew you could talk. Come with me, Joss. I've got something to show you.'

He went to his desk at the front of the classroom. I followed him at a distance.

'Where's my bag?' said Mr Richards. 'Ah! Here it is, the bugger. Now you just hang on a minute, Joss. Wait till you see this.'

He hauled the scruffy holdall up from under the desk and fished around in it.

'Wait a second...aha. Here they are.'

He brought out a polythene bag with some lumpy objects inside, wrapped in what looked like kitchen roll.

'I went metal detecting at the weekend,' he said. 'A lot of rubbish of course. There always is. But I found these as well. Just you look.'

He unwrapped the kitchen roll and showed me.

'Look,' he said.

They were coins, battered and bent and about the size of our five pences. You could just about see the faded inscriptions on them through the dirt. Leofric had had some just like these. I strained my brain to think of the word he'd used for them.

'Coins,' Mr Richards said. He sounded awed, as if he was talking about the Crown Jewels. 'Coins, like the ones you and your friends put in the Coke machine at break times. Boys like you, a thousand years ago. They'd have held them in their hands, just like we're doing now. Don't you think that's fantastic? History in the palm of your hand.'

I couldn't work out for the life of me what he was getting so excited about. It seemed like stating the obvious to me. And Leofric hadn't held them in his hands. Like everyone else, he'd kept his money in a kind of pouch slung around his middle on a belt.

Suddenly, I got it.

'Sceattas,' I said.

It seemed to jolt him. The teacher talking kindly to the difficult pupil disappeared. He became sharper, more interested.

'What did you say?'

'Sceattas,' I said sullenly, 'that's what they're called. The coins. That's the name for them.'

'I know what they're called, Joss,' he said. 'I'm just a bit...forgive me. I was a bit surprised that you knew. How did you know?'

'I must've read it somewhere,' I said, 'and you don't need to act so surprised. I can *read*, you know.'

He smiled uncertainly, as if I'd made a joke. I was annoyed with myself for letting slip I knew what the coins were called – not that it was a big secret or anything, just that I try very hard not to tell anyone anything, if I can help it.

Mr Richards sat down more firmly at his desk, like someone settling in for the duration.

'I'm from Wales, Joss,' he said, 'miles from home! I miss it, but I can't leave. Well, between you and me, I don't want to leave. Because when you live in Hoxne, the Anglo-Saxon period feels very close at hand, and I wouldn't want to lose that. Do you know what I mean?'

I did, and he had no idea how I did. I missed them all. Leofric, my friend. Merwenna. I even missed Wuffa.

'I suppose so,' I said.

He looked boyishly pleased with my answer, as if he was glad to have found a fellow enthusiast.

'Tell me something,' he said. 'What got you interested in the Anglo-Saxons?'

He gave a short, embarrassed laugh, and passed a hand through what was left of the springy ginger hair.

'Sorry,' he said, 'I'm just not used to students being interested in anything.'

'Why are you? Interested, I mean,' I said.

His eyes beneath their tufted brows lit up.

'They call it the Dark Ages, but that's so.... condescending. They weren't primitives, painting on cave walls,' he said. 'They were a sophisticated and complex people. They had art, a monetary system. Houses we would recognise as being like ours. A social structure at least as complicated as ours. Calling it the Dark Ages is just... plain wrong.'

He looked indignantly at me, like it was my fault.

'They couldn't read or write,' I said, remembering the warm evening under the walnut trees. 'Well, most of them couldn't anyway. Maybe that's why it gets called the Dark Ages. Because nothing was written down.'

The bell went for the start of afternoon school, and I jumped out of my seat. The bell at Easterbrook sounded like a fire alarm, and I still hadn't got used to it. I was glad, though. I'd said more than I'd meant to.

'Got to go,' I said. I picked up my phone and bag and can of drink.

'Yes. All right. Goodbye Joss,' said Mr Richards. He sounded puzzled, like there was a lot more he wanted to ask.

I didn't see him again that day until later on, when school was finished. I was shouldering my way to the bus stop through a crowd of kids, and he came up behind me and caught my arm.

'Joss! A word,' he said.

I stopped, reluctantly. The surging kids made their way around us like water finding its way around a stone.

'I wanted to catch you before you left,' he said. 'I've got a book for you. Since you're so interested in the Anglo-Saxons.'

He ran his hand through his heathery hair and gave me

the book. I looked down at the cover: *Hoxne: A Local Anglo-Saxon History* by Julian Simmonds and G R Richards. A book I would never, in a million years, want to read.

I was conscious of curious glances and a few smirks from the sea of kids around us.

'But wait a minute, I never told you I was interested. I'm not. I'm not interested in Anglo-Saxon history,' I said, but it was too late. Mr Richards had gone, swept away in the tide away from the school entrance. I heard his voice, the Welshness more obvious now he was shouting: 'Year Sevens, stop pushing! Single-file queuing for the buses, *please.*'

൫൫

'There's no getting out of it, not if someone's really determined to lend you a book,' Cressida said.

She was making a cake in the kitchen. *A Local Anglo-Saxon History* lay face up on the table, surrounded by currants and eggs and bags of flour and sugar. Tim picked it up.

'We know him,' he said, 'don't we, Cressida? Julian Simmonds is the vicar. And the Richards chap teaches at Easterbrook.'

'Yeah, I know. He's my class teacher,' I said.

'They had it printed privately. You can buy copies at the post office, and in the library. It did quite well locally, I think.'

He dusted flour off the cover.

'Can I borrow it? I'd like to read it.'

'Yeah, take it. I'm not going to read it,' I said.

I felt sour and empty, and sourer and emptier with every day that went past. Alice hardly looked in my direction at school, and who could blame her? She pointedly sat well away from me on the bus. And one night, I had a peculiar, complicated dream about her and Merwenna; they were muddled up and interchangeable and, in the strange way of dreams, you couldn't tell which one was which. I woke up tangled in the sheets, sweating and dry-mouthed with longing. I couldn't even text Harry Fraser or anyone in Ipswich because I'd run out of credit days ago and anyway I didn't have anything to say to them. I didn't have anything to say to anyone.

'Come and help me in the greenhouse. We've just got time to water the tomatoes and pick the ripe ones before church,' Tim said.

'I'm not going to church,' I said.

Tim laughed. 'I know that. I meant we as in Cressida and me. Come on.'

The greenhouse sat on the edge of the lawn, in full sun. It was sauna-hot inside, and full of a green, jungly smell which Tim said was the tomatoes. He switched on a little radio and some tinny voices started talking away to each other. Tim had his back to me; he was leaning over the bench doing something with pots of earth.

'Pass me the tomato feed, would you, Joss? The red and green bottle,' he said.

I felt comfortable and easy, and suddenly like I wanted to talk to him. Which I knew I wouldn't have felt if he'd been sitting squarely facing me, carefully empathising with me by mirroring my body language, like they taught you in college, like Sofia always did, and all the other social workers and teachers and educational psychologists and school nurses. There must have been dozens of them over the years, and there is nothing more likely to make me shut up like a clam than a pair of beady eyes looking at me and a Listening expression.

'I miss Tracy. And my sisters,' I said.

'Yes. I know you do.'

Tim's voice was warm and gentle.

'It's not you and Cressida. You're both really kind…but I don't belong here. I feel like I'm from another planet half the time. I'm lonely.'

The sad word 'lonely' made the tears prick at the back of my eyes. Tim reached behind for the watering can, and I put it into his hand.

'That nice girl. Alice. Could you talk to her, do you think?'

'No. Not any more…not ever, really.'

'That's hard,' Tim said.

'It doesn't have to be! It doesn't have to be this hard. It's not a, a, a…natural law that I have to be here. The world wouldn't end if I went back to Ipswich. It's bloody Sofia. Bloody social workers, writing their reports, full of words like 'appropriate' and 'child-centred'. It's a different language, and if you're like Tracy and don't speak it, you've got no chance.'

Tim moved from plant to plant, watering.

'It isn't her fault. Sofia. She's not the reason this happened.'

'You think it's Tracy's fault. It is, I suppose,' I said.

He turned round from the plants and handed me the watering can.

'There, I've finished,' he said, 'and I don't think that. Let he who is without sin cast the first stone.'

'You only say that,' I said furiously, 'because it says it in the bloody Bible. It's just *words*. You don't mean it.'

Tim put an earthy hand on my shoulder.

'Sorry. Didn't mean to be sanctimonious. But it's true. We shouldn't beat each other up for things – none of us is perfect! And most things don't matter as much as we think they do. We're just little animals running about on a planet. Not as important as we think we are.'

I felt my anger begin to drain away like water down a plughole. And it hadn't been him I was angry with anyway.

'You better go,' I said, 'Cressida's wearing a funny hat and waving at you. Must be church time.'

It was half past ten and the church bells were still ringing when someone came knocking at the door.

It was Alice.

I stared at her, knowing with complete certainty that

she'd picked her moment, waiting till Cressida and Tim had gone, to catch me on my own. It depressed me. It made her seem little and petty, and I didn't want to think of her like that.

'Hello, Joss. I wondered if you wanted to come for a walk with me,' she said.

Her loveliness almost knocked me out. She shone with health. There had never been such perfect skin before.

I didn't answer at first. I couldn't even look at her in the face for more than about a second. I felt pulled in about six different directions at once: Alice and her glossy hair and sister at Jesus (*'it's in Cambridge, Joss'*); the uncomfortable, dangerous world of Merwenna and Leofric; Cressida and Tim and their big house and mad clothes; Tracy and my sisters and the hot, familiar lounge in Ipswich with the telly on and people coming and going all the time, the friendly fug of cigarettes and the closing fist of asthma in my chest. Home.

The clashing of the different worlds made me furious.

'No, I can't. I'm busy. Sorry,' I said.

I watched as her shoulders slumped and the smile drained out of her face.

I closed the door before I could feel any worse. From the hall window, I could see her trail slowly back up the drive. I pictured her taking out her phone, getting a signal and phoning Rufus Palmier-Thompson for a shoulder to cry on, now I'd been such a dick to her. It was only me thinking it, but I was as bitter and angry as if she'd actually done it.

When she'd gone, I sat around in the house and then,

after a while, I couldn't bear my own bitterness any more, so I borrowed one of Tim's peculiar sun hats from the peg in the greenhouse and set out for a walk.

The sun poured down like honey. A heat haze hung over the fields, and the air seemed too hot even for the birds to sing. I took off my T and tucked it into the waistband of my jeans. I hadn't put on sun cream, but I have the kind of skin that doesn't need it.

I walked through a stubbly field of some crop or other, and then turned towards the church, which sat in a kind of hollow down and to my right. I had a vague idea about meeting Cressida and Tim. The quarry – a deep yellowish scar cutting through the green – lay about a half a kilometre beyond the church. I must have cycled around in a great, pointless circle that night.

The warmth of the sun had made me less angry, and I sat down on a bench in the churchyard. I could hear the singing of the people inside the church. Cressida and Tim, singing their hearts out.

There was something so peaceful about the scene, the church with its stubby little spire prodding upwards, planted between trees and fields and under the hot blue bowl of the sky. If you wanted to picture England, this was what you would think of. Even the fact that the church was being renovated along one side and there were tools and a cement mixer sitting about, as well as orange builder's tape stretching everywhere; even all that couldn't stop it being pretty. The sun drenched everything with warm, clear light. It seemed ridiculous that I wasn't happy.

I became aware of someone near me and looked up to see a man sitting on a bench against the wall of the church and reading a newspaper. He was wearing square-framed glasses and drinking orange juice from a carton.

He felt me looking at him, tucked the paper under his arm and smiled.

'Haven't seen you round here before, have I?'

'Probably not,' I said cautiously. He didn't look like a lunatic, but you can never tell.

'Hot, isn't it? I'm Julian Simmonds. I'm the vicar,' he said.

'The *vicar?*'

I must have sounded incredulous, because he smiled, showing teeth that were endearingly crooked.

'Well, yes. Someone's got to be. The curate's doing the service, I thought it was too nice to be cooped up. Come and have a cold drink – the vicarage is just over there.'

'No, thanks,' I said, 'I'm waiting for Cressida and Tim, and anyway, my mother told me never to talk to strange men.'

He laughed a hooty laugh.

'Very commendable of her. And you must be Cressida and Tim's latest guest. Welcome to Hoxne.'

He was wearing a shabby grey sweatshirt and baggy grey joggers, which made him look more like someone on remand than a vicar. His hair, though short, stuck up all over the place. I couldn't see a dog collar, but maybe he was one of those cool, modern vicars who didn't wear them. You wouldn't have been surprised to see odd socks underneath the grey joggers.

His name seemed familiar, and then a light dawned.

'*A Local Anglo-Saxon History*. You wrote it,' I said.

He actually blushed.

'Have you read it?' he said.

'I've *got* it,' I said.

He sat on the bench next to me.

'I love the history of places. This place we're sitting, for example. It was here a thousand years ago, and it'll be here in another thousand. Makes you think, doesn't it?'

I made an indeterminate noise.

'That's what history is, of course. Real people, just like you and me. Different clothes, different things to eat and worry about, but fundamentally just the same.'

'Um. Yes,' I said. He had no idea of how much I knew what he meant. And it reminded me of something that Tim had been saying that morning, watering the tomatoes in the jungle air of the greenhouse.

'Of course, the Anglo-Saxon history of Hoxne, at this distance, it's almost unknowable. Which makes it even more interesting. Unknowable in the same way that God's unknowable. You never expect to know the ins and outs of God, do you?'

I really, really hoped he wasn't going to start going on about God, because it makes me go hot and cold when people do that, so to shut him up I asked, abruptly, if actually I could have a drink of water.

☙❧

CHAPTER ELEVEN

❧

svarraði-sàrgymir
wound-sea (literal translation)

BLOOD

❧

I followed him through the gravestones and through a gate into the garden of the vicarage, which was a modern, square house with orange bricks and bright white plastic window frames. It looked out of place next to the stone church. We went into the kitchen, and Julian told me the story of Edmund, and the battle at Hoxne against the Vikings. What happened was this.

Following years of lightning raids on the coasts and up and down the rivers, the Danes invaded Anglo-Saxon England properly for the first time in 865. By the winter of the year, they'd reached East Anglia and camped there for the winter. Probably, Julian said, in what is now Thetford.

The leader of the Viking army was called Ivar the Boneless. Julian didn't know why he was called this. Maybe he was fat or something. Anyway, he and his brother Ubba (just Ubba. He didn't seem to have a nickname) wintered more or less peacefully in Thetford with their army, and then the Anglo-Saxons provided them with money and horses, in exchange for an agreement that there wouldn't be an attack on East Anglia. They tried to buy them off, in other words. Ivar the Boneless kept his word, sort of, and in 866 the Viking army marched north, away from East Anglia. They fought their way up the spine of England to York, destroying villages and towns and churches and monasteries. Then they turned round and headed south, pausing in 867 in Nottingham for a bit more destruction before the Mercians there caved in and surrendered. By the late summer of 869, the Vikings were poised to attack East Anglia.

This time, Julian said, there wasn't any attempt by Edmund, the King of the East Anglians, to buy them off. Perhaps he had run short of money, or maybe the Viking army was so strong by now that they knew they could defeat him, and would ignore or reject any proposed bargaining. Or maybe Edmund had simply resolved to resist them. Nobody knows for sure, but what is known is that during the late autumn of 869, the Viking army attacked, and crushed the resistance put up by Edmund's army.

It was a bloodbath, Julian said.

On the 20th of November, Edmund was killed at Hoxne. There were quite a few accounts of this, some contemporary and some written later, and they all agreed on the date. After he was dead, there was nothing to stop Ivar and his Danish army. They overran the kingdom.

Julian poured me a glass of water and switched the kettle on.

'Tea?' I asked. 'It's about a million degrees outside.'

'But drinking hot liquids speeds up heat loss. Because of evaporation. Why do you think they eat curry in India?'

'Don't know.' I said, 'Maybe because the meat goes off. Because it's so hot there.'

Julian fished in one of his two dishwashers for a teaspoon.

'Well,' he said, 'maybe that's another reason. There's usually more than one reason for things.'

Julian's kitchen was like Julian himself: messy and haphazard, and more than a little peculiar. The dishwashers were one thing. I mean, who has two dishwashers? And it looked like a kitchen that had been put together quickly from the remnants of other kitchens; the units were different colours and styles, and looked like they'd been hammered into place by someone who hadn't had a lot of time. Nothing matched. Even the floor tiles changed from reddish where we were, sitting at the table, to a kind of cream colour as they approached the back door.

I cleared my throat.

'This King Edmund,' I said, 'he sounds pretty bloody useless to me. Bribing them to go away...that's not going to work more than once, is it? And then losing the fight and getting found under a bridge.'

'Well, the odds were overwhelmingly against him,' Julian

said. 'It's hard to see how they could ever have won. And the bridge story is only a legend.'

'*Legend*. As in not true.'

Julian poured tea from a fat brown teapot into a pink pint mug.

'Sure you won't have some tea?'

I shook my head. 'No thanks. I don't really like tea to be honest, Julian. It wasn't true then, was it, about the bridge?'

He smiled, like a teacher encouraging a pupil who's trying hard to understand. 'It depends what you mean by "true". Legends and fairy tales often have their basis in truth. But most historians agree it isn't fundamentally true. As in, exactly what happened.'

Through the open window, you could hear the sharp, urgent cries of seagulls. I didn't know you got them this far inland. I pictured Alice, how she'd looked when she was telling me about it being bad luck to cross the bridge on the way to your wedding: eyes slitted against the sun and that sleepy cat smile. *Alice*. Her name passed across my heart, leaving a long, stinging scratch.

I swallowed.

'What happened, according to the legend, I mean?'

'It's rather interesting,' Julian said. 'The legend is that after losing the battle, Edmund was hiding under the bridge in Hoxne. His gold armour was reflected in the water, and a couple on their way to get married spotted it and shopped him to the Vikings. It's called the Goldbrook legend because of the...'

'Reflection, yeah, I see. It all sounds a bit unlikely.'

Julian put the pink mug back down on the table. He had drunk a pint of hot tea on a scorching day in about a minute. His insides must be made of asbestos.

'Unlikely things happen all the time,' he said.

No, what happens all the time is people saying things like that. Like legends and fairy tales not being *fundamentally true*. Like Cressida saying 'it'll be all right' when she couldn't possibly know.

'Gold armour,' I said contemptuously, 'even kings wouldn't wear gold armour. And why the hell would anyone be getting married in the middle of a battle? And no one would shop their own king.' I remembered Wuffa, and his vicious spit onto the ground. 'They hated the Vikings. They were their deadliest enemies.'

'You're quite right, Sherlock,' Julian said, 'full of holes and very unlikely.' He smiled. He had a crooked smile, further down on one side than the other.

'Any particular reason? For your interest.'

I wondered what he would say if I told him. Ring the hospital, probably, and have me sectioned. Instead, I repeated what Mr Richards had said, about the Dark Ages being the wrong name for people who were just as clever and cultured and complicated as we were, only in a different way.

'Well, of course,' Julian said. He sounded surprised. 'Why wouldn't they be? They were people, like you and me. Why wouldn't they like art and music and nice clothes? Of course they did, they were from a different time, that's all. Not a different species.'

I drank the rest of my water and stood up.

'Will church have finished?' I asked. 'Only I was going to meet Cressida and Tim.'

Julian looked up at the clock on the wall – hexagonal in shape, orange plastic and printed with the words WHYTE AND MACKAY.

'Probably,' he said. 'Depends how long-winded Stephen's been. Stephen's the curate. Come on, let's go and see if he's finished.'

We went outside, and Stephen had evidently wound it up because people were coming out of the church into the bright sunlight. I thought I glimpsed Cressida's strange hat bobbing about two or three rows back in the dim church interior. She and Tim would be out any moment.

Julian said he'd better go and shake some hands.

'All right,' I said, 'I'll wait for Tim and Cressida.'

The sight of the peculiar bobbing hat had made me want to smile. Suddenly, I was almost happy, despite the fact that tomorrow was Monday and it'd be back to Easterbrook and Alice, or rather not-Alice because she wouldn't even look at me after today, would she, and who could blame her?

The teachers at Easterbrook were on the whole the same as the ones at the dump-school in Ipswich; like at the bus stop that first morning, you could sort them into types even if you didn't know them at all. People are people. I put up with them, the way you do when you've not been given any choice.

From Mrs Watts (geography), I put up with Pleading Flattery: 'You're such a smart boy, Joss. If only you applied yourself.' From Mr Deakin (resistant materials) I put up with Man to Man Chumminess: 'Look, lad, do 'A' levels, work hard and then you can tell the lot of us to go to hell.' From Mr Norton (maths), I put up with Offended Outrage: 'Don't bother then, Joss. See if I care when you end up on the scrapheap.'

I endured it all without saying anything in return. And then on Monday afternoon, I was summoned to Ms Osborne's office and I got ready to endure some more, only what she had for me was different and even worse. As the blow fell, I realised I'd been waiting for it, or something like it, ever since the day I left Ipswich in Sofia's shiny blue social worker's car.

Tracy had taken an overdose.

Ms Osborne talked to me in a stupid voice, a voice loaded down with Sympathy and Patience and Understanding.

I said nothing.

I hated her so much, I could hardly speak.

She'd done it before – Tracy, I mean – a couple of years ago when the twins were really little. I'd come home and found her on the floor of the bathroom, covered in sick. I'd come home early because I was bored, and it was a good thing I did, because otherwise she would have died.

'Joss?' Ms Osborne said.

Her lizard face was tilted to one side. Sympathy and

Understanding.

'I'm going home,' I said.

A flash of irritation showed in the reptilian eyes.

'You can't, I'm afraid. There isn't a bus to Hoxne till the end of school. And if you're talking about Ipswich, that's something you'll have to talk about with your social worker. With Ms Bassett-Torres. You can wait in the—'

'Then I'll fucking walk,' I said.

In the end, Mr Richards gave me a lift. He'd been hanging round in the corridor outside Ms Osborne's office, not quite whistling and leaning on a lamp post, but obviously waiting and pretending that he wasn't.

He offered to drive me back to Hoxne, and he didn't say a word while we were driving. Which I was grateful for; any more phoney sympathy and I might've puked, only you didn't actually feel with Mr Richards that it would be phoney necessarily.

'Down here,' I said. 'House by the tree.'

He pulled into the crunchy drive and stopped by the front door.

'Try not to worry. None of this'll matter at all in a thousand years,' he said.

'I know. But what about tomorrow? I don't care what happens in a thousand years,' I said.

'I know. It's hard.'

He was getting Welsher by the minute.

'I just feel so helpless. I know they mean well…I suppose they do, but they make everything worse. And there's nothing I can do to make it better, and that's driving me mad. Stuck here, I can't do anything to make a *difference*.'

My mouth was dry, however much I swallowed.

'And it'll rumble on without me – they'll put the girls up for adoption if they decide to. Tracy'll go further and further down the plughole. Take me with her, I expect… and there's nothing I can do. You just have to watch the car crash coming closer, just totally helpless.'

I didn't know where all that came from. I hadn't planned it; it had just poured out of me like I'd opened a vein or something.

He sighed. 'I know, it must be a terrible feeling. But you said it, Joss, there's nothing you can do.'

I shook my head. I wanted to howl my frustration at the blindness that couldn't see it was the loss of her children that had driven Tracy to take her overdose, not the other way round. That her stupid, desperate, defiant act might lead to them being taken away permanently was insane. It was so insane, I wanted to cry.

Instead, I opened the car door.

'Right. Thanks for the lift.'

'No problem. Take care, Joss,' Mr Richards said.

He drove off with a scrunch of gravel, and I went into the house.

Cressida was on the phone, and I could tell from her face who she was talking to.

She covered the mouthpiece with her hand. 'It's Sofia.

Did they tell you...'

'Yeah. They did.'

I took the phone, and heard Sofia's tinny voice tell me that they would need to rethink the care package for Virginia and Sylvia, that they needed to be sure Tracy was capable of looking after herself as well as little children, that they needed to be sure about the state of her emotional wellbeing...

It went on and on, and I held the phone away from my ear. I was so furious my whole body throbbed with it.

It was too much to hear. I dropped the phone back into its cradle, and cut off the poisonous, jangly little voice, saying things I couldn't bear to hear and couldn't do anything to change.

Cressida squeezed my shoulder. In the dim light of the hallway, the shapeless dress she wore dripped off her like a dust sheet. The diamonds she wore in her ears flashed like tiny lasers.

'Don't think about it any more. Don't torture yourself for nothing. Go out into the garden, Tim's there somewhere. And Julian.'

The Reverend Julian Simmonds.

'I don't need any spiritual guidance from Julian,' I said, trying and failing to make a joke.

She squeezed my shoulder again. 'Tell them I'm bringing cold drinks out,' she said.

☉☉

The two of them were lying in deckchairs under a tree, looking like caricatures on an old-fashioned postcard. You could imagine knotted handkerchiefs and rolled-up trouser legs, although in fact both of them were wearing straw hats and shorts.

Their four white, whiskery legs stuck out over the grass like the legs of some peculiar jointed insect.

'Your other half gave me a lift home,' I said to Julian.

'My other…oh, you mean the book. Gordon. G R Richards.'

He watched me benignly from underneath the big straw hat.

'Yeah. Julian, tell me something. If you could go back in time, you know, to Anglo-Saxon Hoxne, what would you take with you?'

He looked interested.

'Ah, a balloon-debate question. Like the Wells Time Machine. Which three books would you take with you into a future world?'

Tim cleared his throat. I thought he might be about to start talking about books, *David Copperfield* or something, and I didn't want that. I had a sudden panicky feeling that there wasn't much time.

I wanted to go back. I wanted to be with Merwenna and Leofric and Aesc, because their lives were real and true and necessary, keen and essential as the blade of a knife. I didn't care that they were all buried in a thousand years of history. I didn't even care if they weren't real. Even if I'd imagined the whole thing, I'd rather be there, in their hard, muddy, dangerous world, than here in mine.

At least in Haegelisdun there might be half a chance of actually making a difference.

And if I was going back to Haegėlisdun, I would need to think about what I was going to take with me. There must be a way to exploit the thousand years of technological advances that separated us. Obviously, I knew we now had nuclear weapons and tanks and landmines, but that was countries, not people. As a private individual, I seemed to have gone backwards not forwards. I was far less use than Leofric or Aesc when it came to fighting Vikings. I was probably less use in a battle than Merwenna.

'I don't mean books. I meant useful things – weapons. Things to help you win a war.'

'What an interesting question, Joss,' Tim said. His eyes asked the follow-up question: why was I asking? I shrugged my shoulders, and squinted up at the sky, hard and bright as a mirror with heat.

'Do you know,' Julian said gently, 'I don't think I would take any weapons. I mean, even if you could get your hands on some Semtex or, I don't know, a machine gun, would that really terrify a Viking? It'd be a new way of killing, but they're used to killing.'

He was right, I realised. 'What, then?' I said.

Tim scrambled upright in his deckchair.

'Julian's right. I'd take something that would stop them in their tracks. Something that would astound them, take their breath away. Imagine a ninth-century man looking at an aeroplane! Even a little Cessna; they wouldn't believe it – it'd scare them silly.'

I saw what they meant, but I had even less chance of obtaining a Cessna than I did of getting a machine gun.

Cressida came out with a tray of strawberries and the stuff she called lemonade, although she made it herself in a tin bucket in the kitchen and it was yellow and sharp, not fizzy and clear like the lemonade Tracy bought for the twins.

'Cold drinks, Joss,' she said, 'and try not to worry. It'll be all right.'

That night, I made a list.

Two-way radios

Antibiotics and painkillers

BB guns/air rifles

Fireworks

Nylon rope

Stuff for making petrol bombs

Julian had said the battle at Hoxne had been a bloodbath, and I thought the petrol bombs might help us fight at a distance, which would certainly be the way I'd prefer to do it. And the BB guns for the same reason. They were the closest thing I could think of to actual firearms. The radios I thought would come in useful for keeping a lookout for invaders, although God knows how I would persuade Penda and Wuffa to use them. I remembered how deeply suspicious the doctor – what was his name? –

had been of my inhalers. And I'd put rope because it was easy – I could wind it round my waist or something – and because the ones they used in Haegelisdun, the ones they made out of nettles, weren't all that strong and used to break all the time. Fireworks weren't much compared to the miracle of powered flight, but then you can't exactly tuck a Cessna under your arm and carry it. I hoped they'd be astonishing and terrifying enough. I knew the Chinese had invented them in the year dot; I just hoped the news of the invention hadn't spread to Scandinavia. As for the medicines, I didn't want to think about why I needed to take them. Tracy told me once about my great grandad – or maybe it was a few more greats – who'd got through the First World War, came home and died of infected wounds about six months later. It had always struck me as a pretty sad and pointless way to die.

I lay on my back on my bed and ran through the list in my head.

I wondered if I'd missed something.

I wondered if it would be enough.

I wondered if I'd be able to carry it all, even.

I thought about it obsessively, over and over, until I was almost asleep, because that way it meant I didn't have to think about Tracy and Virginia and Sylvia, and what was going to happen next.

⊚⊚

CHAPTER TWELVE

✪✪

gold-þeof
gold stealer (literal translation)

THIEF

✪✪

I caught the bus into Ipswich and spent all the money
I had, and some of Cressida's that I'd borrowed, at the
Firework Emporium on Haylings Road. I used Harry
Fraser's fake ID, which I'd forgotten to give back to him
when I left. Rockets and roman candles, Catherine wheels
and cherry bombs. I had to steal the two-way radios from
a little electrical shop on a back street in Whatton. I don't
like stealing things, and I only do it when, like now, there
isn't any other way. I wanted really good ones, not crackling
kids' toys that would fade out at vital moments, and I
didn't have enough money in my account for good ones.
And I couldn't have taken any more money from Cressida

and Tim. Even though it would have been easy: they left it lying around all the time – jars full of change, £10 notes stuffed into teapots; that kind of thing.

I did take some matches from the kitchen though, and two full petrol cans I found in the garage. I found some rope there too, and an air rifle Tim kept for shooting rabbits. It looked ancient, but I took it anyway, and some pellets I found in a biscuit tin on a shelf nearby. The scraps of material for making petrol-bomb fuses I found in Cressida's sewing basket.

After we'd eaten, I told Cressida and Tim that I wanted an early night and went upstairs to my room, where I piled everything into the wardrobe in my room so it would be out of sight. They never came in, but I wasn't taking any chances. And as I jammed the wardrobe door shut, I wondered what the hell I thought I was doing.

I felt like a child, pretending.

I felt like an actor must feel, sitting in a room putting on a false beard and crown to go and be King Lear in front of an audience.

I felt like an idiot, but feeling like an idiot was better than the emptiness there'd be if this was all there was.

I was going back to Haegelisdun. And I was going back to help.

෧෧

Luckily for me, one of the little shops by the village green was a pharmacy. It really was a massive bit of luck, because there were only about six shops in the whole of Hoxne, if you included the post office, and two of them sold stupid, random, expensive things like distressed wicker furniture and copper kettles and tin boxes with BREAD stamped on them.

I left the pharmacy till last because I knew getting away wouldn't be the walk in the park it had been at the back-street shop in Whatton.

There was no point in hanging around. There were two days till the end of school. Alice acted like she didn't know who I was. Sofia was coming to see me any day now to let me know what they'd decided about whether I could carry on living with my mother and sisters in the future. I felt like I already knew what that decision would be, and that there was nothing I could do to influence it.

There was nothing here worth staying for.

I went quietly downstairs and out into the front garden. The packed rucksack was digging into my shoulders like the claws of cats.

The warm night air touched my skin with the softness of moths. The garden was drenched in a colourless moonlight.

It took a long time to walk to the village, and I was bent almost in half by the time I got there. You could hear the petrol sloshing inside the cans in the rucksack.

Breaking and entering: I'd done it before but never on my own, and this was different because it was the real thing, not just kids messing about, and my hands were shaking. Not only my hands, but my arms all the way up past my elbows almost to my shoulders.

But it wasn't hard; all I had to do was climb the fence into the little yard at the back of the pharmacy and cautiously break the glass of the window there. It was a small window, so it was a squeeze getting in, but I am skinny and I managed. I cut my hand a bit on the broken glass but I was so breathless and wound-up I hardly noticed. I had to leave the rucksack in the yard. You couldn't have fitted through even a normal door with that on your back.

It was a sort of back room used for storage; the dispensary was the next room along. I used one of Tim's screwdrivers to force the lock. And that was easy enough too, but as soon as the wood splintered around the lock and I stepped inside, the alarm went off, just like I knew it would.

It was a scream that grew and grew until it filled my whole head. My teeth were ringing with the noise as I flashed the torch around the shelves and swept amoxycillin, penicillin and flucloxacillin into the satchel I wore slantwise across my chest. Painkillers: I found paracetamol and codeine and then I forced open the controlled drugs cabinet and took handfuls of boxes: morphine sulphate and Oramorph and co-dyadramol. There was injectable stuff as well, but I didn't take it. I waved the torch around wildly a few times but I couldn't see any needles or anything, and there wasn't time to look properly.

Oh, God, that demented alarm. Get out of here. Get out of here! I slashed my other hand on more broken glass struggling out through the store-room window, and then I was back in the fresh, pure air of the warm outdoors night, with the scream of the alarm going through me like nails through flesh and wood. I heaved the rucksack onto my back and climbed onto the dustbins to get over the fence. I could hear the anxious murmur of voices, the beginnings of a stirring in the houses nearest to the pharmacy.

I headed up the hill to the quarry. The quarry, my accidental gateway to Haegelisdun. Keep going. Keep going. I must keep going. The stupid word 'portal' got into my brain and lodged there.

But the voices were getting louder and closer, audible now, just under the screeching alarm.

I kept running, one foot in front of another, and tried not to hear them.

Until I was there, standing at the lip of the quarry, almost – as far as I could tell in those wild panting seconds – at the point where I'd somersaulted over the handlebars of Tim's bike that night. There was a pain in my chest like a knife, and every breath in was flavoured with blood.

Hoxne was behind me, with its one street light and the footsteps of people coming to see what all the noise was. And all I could hear was my own panting breath and the burglar alarm, which had somehow got tangled up with the swish and roar of my own heartbeats pumping in my ears.

All I had to do was jump.

But I was afraid; afraid of taking a step out into thin air; afraid of my own fear. Afraid of it not working. That was what scared me most. I knew, suddenly and for the first time, that I didn't actually believe that it would.

I stood there like an idiot, bent low under the weight of that bloody rucksack, and my chest squeezing itself tighter and tighter in an effort to drag in air. I couldn't do it. I couldn't step sweetly off the edge of the quarry into nothingness. I didn't believe it, and I wasn't strong enough to trust it without believing.

The sound of people behind me crystallised into voices: just a general clamour at first then proper speech, a soundbite close enough for me to hear the words: 'Over here, I think! This way!'

I couldn't do it. I stepped painfully away from the edge of the quarry and set off running again.

I ran to the church. Not deliberately, because by now I had lost any sense of direction, but I found myself retracing my steps across a field of wheat or corn or whatever and arriving in front of the stubby black outline of Julian's church. Julian's house leant up against it, one light showing in an upstairs window. I heard a telephone start ringing in one of the rooms.

Churches in Ipswich were always kept locked and bolted – I knew this because sometimes me and Harry Fraser and the others used to try getting inside one if it was cold or raining or something. But the door of Julian's church opened easily with just a small creak, and then I was inside, with my breath tearing at me and a stitch pain in my side that felt like it might split me open like a grape any minute. I shut the heavy door behind me, breathed in the damp, dusty, churchy air, and it felt safer.

All I had to do was keep quiet and wait for the fuss to die down and everyone to go home to bed. I had a foolish urge to curl into a ball, to squeeze my eyes shut and shove my fingers in my ears.

Instead there was the murmur of voices outside in the porch and then another soundbite of clear speech: 'Go inside and get him. I'm sure he's in…'

I swept around with my torch. There wasn't much to see, just pools of grey light here and there from the high windows, and the occasional glint of something shiny. I staggered up the aisle, away from the door. I'd been wrong to think of the church as a safe place to hide.

It was a trap.

From the porch outside, more voices: 'Inside, Julian. Careful, I can smell petrol!'

So could I, and when I flashed my torch back towards the door, I could see it: a large, dark pool of liquid on the tiled floor. The cans must have cracked, or maybe the lids had come off when I was running or clambering over fences. Either way, that was it for the petrol-bomb idea.

In the beam of light from the torch, I saw that the church door was slowly opening inwards.

'Keep back,' I said, 'keep bloody back or I'll…I'll light a bloody match and drop it in the petrol.'

'Joss? Is that you?'

It was Julian's voice.

'Go away!' I said. 'Just leave me alone. Don't open that fucking door.'

The thing was, I liked Julian. I'd liked him from the first

moment I met him in the churchyard because there was something about him that you could trust, like he wouldn't have enough guile or cunning to want to lie to you. But at that moment, I hated him. I hated him, and Hoxne, and its interfering, caring villagers. All I wanted was to be left alone. And the other thing that was choking me up inside was that I'd believed, just for a short while, that it was possible to get back to the world of Merwenna and Haegelisdun, a world where things mattered and were real and what you did and said could make a difference. I'd been stupid and wrong. I should have known this unfair mess and muddle was all there was.

'Don't open that fucking door,' I said again, 'or I'll light a match and burn the whole place down. I'll do it. You come any closer, and I'll do it.'

I tried to mean it. I did mean it, only there was a tremor in my voice that enraged me when I heard it. My hands were shaking, but I managed to fish in my pocket for the matches.

The door clunked shut.

'It's all right, Joss. I won't come in, if you don't want me to. But can't you talk to me about what's bothering you?'

'God! You sound like Sofia…like all of them. Just piss off and leave me alone. I don't want any more of that rubbish.'

He hadn't sounded like Sofia at all. For a second, I wondered if it might, by some miracle, be possible to tell him about what I was trying to do. About Haegelisdun. If I could talk to anyone, it would be untidy, shambling king of the dishwashers Julian Simmonds before anyone else.

But then the door creaked again, and the slight softness that had crept into me hardened into ice. I turned and ran down the aisle again, and onto a kind of platform at the end. There was a step up I didn't see in the dark, and I tripped and fell.

I had no idea whether Julian had come into the church and only the dimmest idea, really, of why I was running from him.

There was a click, and the lights came on. The church interior sprang into surprised life, bright after the darkness with whitewashed walls and carved, hard pews in empty lines. The glinty things that had flashed in the torchlight were gold-coloured crosses and a couple of candlesticks.

I couldn't see Julian though.

I'd read somewhere that you should never go into a place you don't know the way out of, and I knew now it was true. There was a mob of people waiting outside armed with expressions of Concern and Worry, but as far as I was concerned, they might as well have been waving pitchforks and carrying flaming torches.

And then I saw Julian. He'd been in a sort of curtained-off alcove by the door, switching the lights on, I guessed. He was wearing a shabby purple dressing gown over pyjamas. And he was saying something, but the drumming of blood in my ears was so loud I couldn't hear what it was.

I was trapped.

I was trapped, just like I had always been. And then I saw it, a wooden door set at the end of the white plaster wall to my right.

It was bound to be locked...and yet it wasn't, and I went through into a little room set out as a kitchen with a sink and a microwave and a kettle. The air smelt of cleaning stuff, overlaid with a stronger smell of damp than there had been in the proper church. Somebody had folded a blue dishcloth tidily over the tap, and it had dried to the shape of an inverted U. There was a key in the lock on this side of the door, but even after I'd locked myself in, and jammed a chair under the door handle, I felt desperate. And a moment later, there was the soft, inevitable knock on the door.

'For God's sake, leave me alone,' I shouted.

His reply came through the door, around the level of my belly. I pictured him stooped to speak through the keyhole.

'I can't. Even if I wanted to, I couldn't, it's my church. But anyway, you're my friend. Why did you break into the pharmacy, Joss? You don't seem like a druggie to me.'

'I'm not one,' I said.

And then there was another sound, quietly and in the background at first, but getting louder and more and more insistent.

A police siren.

I closed my eyes against it. I wanted to concentrate so hard it would all dissolve away: the police, Julian, the mass of concerned villagers outside the door; all the social workers I'd seen in my life; all the youth workers and family therapists, and educational support people. There must have been hundreds of them over the years. If I concentrated hard enough, they might all float away like smoke.

And Tracy and her hopeless inadequate friends, their lives an endless muddle of debt and disaster and one crisis after another. I wanted them all to dissolve away to nothing. I had had enough. Enough.

I could think of nothing but the single word 'please'. It swelled through me to the ends of my fingertips, a whole-body ache that left no room for anything else.

Please.

The door handle turned and rattled as Julian tried to open it. The police siren was still wailing, urgent and close and impossible to ignore.

'You need to open the door, Joss. If you don't open it, we'll have to break it open.'

Please.

I shucked the rucksack off my shoulders, and it crunched heavily on the floor. The 'please' running through my brain was so enormous I couldn't remember why I'd thought I needed all those things.

I climbed up onto the sink and opened the window. It was small, but I could manage. It also gave onto the builder's renovations, but that couldn't be helped either.

The siren was much louder with the window open. The police must be just outside the church.

I dragged myself up onto the narrow sill, my head still full of this enormous, unfocused 'please', full of wanting something so much I didn't know what it was, and dropped out into the darkness.

◎◎

CHAPTER THIRTEEN

❧❧

sól húsanna
girl of the houses (literal translation)

WIFE

❧❧

The sound of the siren stopped as abruptly as a radio being switched off. I was on my hands and knees in the soft, damp grass, jolted from the fall from the window, and it was so dark I couldn't see my hand in front of my face. I couldn't see the gravestones or the bench or the cement mixer and other builders' stuff that had been piled up against the wall.

Then it struck me that the reason I couldn't see my hand in front of my face was because the light from the church windows had gone out, and so had the light from Julian's house, and the glow of the village beyond the houses.

And then I knew I was back in Haegelisdun. It had

happened. I hadn't been able to believe it would, earlier, hadn't been able to – literally – make what I knew Cressida would call a leap of faith. And yet it had happened, almost without me thinking about it. The fierce longing that had swamped me had gone, dissolved painlessly away, and I was full of this enormous gladness.

It had happened.

For once in my life, I had wanted to do something, and it had happened.

It wasn't simply the blackness and the silence that told me I was back. It was the fact that it had been a warm, star-speckled July night, warm enough even at two in the morning not to wear a coat, and now it was cold and damp, with a black starless and moonless sky pressing down overhead. Already, I was shivering. I got up and tested my weight on my legs. No damage, which seemed like more than I could have hoped for. And as soon as I stood up, I realised I was wearing the leggings and tunic combination of Anglo-Saxon Haegelisdun. I was back. I'd done it.

I'd done it, but things hadn't exactly gone to plan. I pictured Tim's rucksack sitting in the little kitchen, and the pools of petrol on the floor of the church. All I had with me was the rope wound round my waist and a satchel full of painkillers and antibiotics. The cold was starting to make my chest tighten and hurt, but in spite of that, I could feel myself smiling. I was back. I was *back*.

I wrapped my arms around myself and set off to find Haegelisdun. Which sounds like it would be easy because how hard can it be to find a whole village of people and animals and houses when you're more or less standing next to it? But the thing is, without light you didn't have any idea which direction to head in. A simple thing like moving from one place to another became a big deal in this profound, silent darkness. No wonder they all went to bed as soon as the sun went down. It was just easier.

I set off walking in the direction I thought was right. I had my arms stretched in front of me like someone sleepwalking, or pretending to be blind, but even so, I kept tripping over lumpy ground and walking into trees. You could hear rustlings and movements all the time in the undergrowth, and the hairs on my neck kept prickling as I pictured eyes watching me as I picked my way through the darkness: Viking eyes or animals – wolves or boars or wildcats. No wonder the Anglo-Saxons built those high wooden walls around their villages. It was to keep the night out, to keep out the unknown and the unseen.

I ended up walking several kilometres to nowhere before I stumbled against the high wall that surrounded Haegelisdun. I felt about with my sleepwalkers' hands and found the ribs of closely fitted wooden stakes, and I knew I was there.

One second later, I was grabbed from behind and my head dragged back by the hair. Somebody had got hold of both my arms and was twisting them back so viciously that it felt like the bones inside were about to snap.

'Cut his throat,' a voice said. 'He doesn't mean any good, creeping about like a thief.'

The voice was curiously uninterested and unexcited, as

if cutting my throat was just one more boring job that had to be done before the end of his shift.

'For God's sake,' I said, 'let go of my bloody arms.'

A knee jammed into the middle of my back, jerking me forward and onto the ground.

'I'm not creeping like a thief,' I said.

I tried to twist round to see who it was that was attacking me, but I got another shove that sent me sprawling face down in the mud.

'He's not a Dane,' another voice said.

'I know, but I don't recognise him. Cut his throat, get it over with. We've got enough to worry about without strangers hanging about.'

'No…I'm not a stranger. I'm looking for Haegelisdun… I've been away. Aesc knows me.'

I wasn't thinking about what I was saying. I was basically just jabbering rubbish. I could feel something cold pressing against my neck and when you're that scared you don't plan what you're going to say; at least I didn't. And I'd never been this terrified before in my life.

I was so frightened, I forgot how to breathe.

The night must have been almost over because pink fingers of sky were beginning to show over the tops of the trees. In the bleached grey light I saw there were three of them, tired-looking men who I guessed had been on sentry duty all night.

'Is this…is it Haegelisdun?'

'Shut your mouth, you spying dog,' said the tallest of the three. He seemed to be in charge because the others looked at him when they asked anything, and he was in charge of me because he was the one pressing the blade of the knife against my neck. I let out an involuntary bleating noise.

'Take him in to Aesc. Fasten his hands behind him so he can't try anything.'

The blade was taken away from my neck.

Breathe. Breathe.

It is surprisingly hard to walk with your hands tied behind your back. I stumbled and tripped every step I took. I was clumsy enough anyway, the mud from all my hours of wandering about earlier was clogged onto my feet and made it feel like I was wearing heavy, sticky moon boots. I had to concentrate to stay upright.

'In here. This way.'

Only one of the sentries came into the village with me. He held the rope that tied my hands and towed me like I was a dog on a lead.

Haegelisdun had changed a lot since I was there last. It was packed with even more people, sleeping in doorways or sitting propped up against the walls of the pigsty. The whole place had the makeshift, haphazard, temporary look of an airport full of stranded passengers. Spears were stacked together in vertical stacks, shields lay in mounds like giant coins. There were smoking remains of fires, with cauldrons suspended over them on tripods, and what looked like clothes in soft heaps. There was a sheen of frost over everything, and bright daggers of ice hanging from the roofs of the houses. My breath hung in the grey early-morning air.

'What day is it? What's the date?' I asked, but the man holding the rope didn't answer, just gave the rope a quick pull, like you might do if your dog wasn't keeping up. He stopped in front of a skinny, matted-haired man who was squatting on his haunches cleaning what looked like a javelin. No; sharpening it.

'Hey. You. Where's Aesc? This stranger claims acquaintance with him. I need to speak to Aesc,' he said.

The skinny man looked up from his sharpening.

'Follow me. And bring the boy with you. I don't want any trouble – he's your responsibility.'

He put down the javelin and got up.

The skin of ice that had formed over the mud cracked and shifted under me as the two of them towed me towards the Great Hall. They knocked on the door, and after a while it opened, and someone came out carrying one of those flame torches you see in films.

It was Wuffa.

He nearly stuck the torch up my nose when he bent forward to look at my face.

'We found this stranger...' began the man who had brought me, but Wuffa interrupted him.

'It's you! We thought we'd seen the last of you. Where have you been hiding yourself since the summer?'

I said nothing. I had forgotten how bulky he was, and how nervous he made me. At the same time, I was overwhelmingly glad to see someone I recognised.

'He claims to know Aesc,' the guard said.

'Yes,' said Wuffa. He was still peering closely at my face as if he needed to make sure it was really me and not some imposter. 'Yes, he's managed to make himself a favourite of Aesc's. I don't know how, but he has.'

He jerked with his thumb towards the rope.

'Cut him loose.'

The knife was slipped between my wrists and cut the nettle rope that tied my hands.

'Come into the hall,' Wuffa said. My feet were numb with the cold, and as I followed him, I tripped. He caught my arm and steadied me.

'Careful,' he said.

The dawn was really breaking now, and the light from the flame torch and the remains of the fires were beginning to look pale and a bit unhealthy, the way lights left on unnecessarily always make things look. My teeth began to chatter together.

'I'm frozen solid,' I said.

I didn't want him to think I was shaking for any other reason than the cold.

To my total astonishment, he plucked a hairy blanket from a pile just outside the door and dumped it over my shoulders.

'Get close to the fire,' he said, just as Aesc had said on my first day in Haegelisdun, 'and mind where you step.'

The Great Hall was being used as a billet. There were wooden cot beds all along the wall, but most of the men were on the floor – a living carpet of sleeping men, wedged with hardly any space between them. You had to step carefully; Wuffa was right. A whole army was in Haegelisdun, I realised. Edmund's army.

'What day is it today?' I said.

'November. The nineteenth of November,' Wuffa said.

He took a couple of logs from a basket nailed halfway up the wall and threw them into the fire.

'You've been gone all of the autumn. But you're back in time for the battle with the Danes.'

'Yeah. Just in time,' I said.

He stared at me, and I dropped my eyes. Last time we'd seen each other, he'd been ranting about how I'd betrayed Leofric. I wanted to say something to him, about how he'd been right about this, but I felt instinctively that it would be wiser to move on. Now was not the moment.

'I have to go,' Wuffa said, 'but I'm glad you're back to fight.'

'Yeah. Me too,' I said.

People were waking up; the fire flared higher and two women came in with a pot which they fixed above the flames. A few minutes later, a soupy, meaty smell began to fill the air. The feeling was coming back into my hands. I took off my shoes and banged the mud off them.

Someone passed me a wooden bowl of soup. Wuffa had gone. I hadn't seen him go, and I could see no one that I recognised. The rough wool curtain was pulled across the entrance to the bower, I noticed, so Aesc was probably inside. I wondered where Leofric was, and whether he was with Merwenna.

One of the men made a space for me on the floor.

'Sit down, youngster. Eat your breakfast.'

The women were opening the shutters, letting in slices of pale dirty light and fresh air. I could see my new friend now, and I saw he had thin grey hair, pulled into a ratty ponytail, and a face full of lines and furrows. He looked about a hundred years old, but I would have bet he wasn't more than forty.

He cleared a space on the ground with a hand like a brown claw.

'For your possessions,' he said.

'I don't think I need that much room. I don't possess much,' I said.

I emptied my satchel and looked sadly at the chemist's boxes with their colourful printing and complicated medical names. No petrol bombs or air rifle or two-way radios. Oh, that bloody rucksack.

'What are those objects?' the man asked.

'I brought them to help. From Gipeswic,' I said. They looked like nothing, tumbled there in a mass on the floor, like children's toys. Lego bricks, or blocks with letters on.

'Some of them take pain away, and some of them stop wounds getting infected. I'll take them to the doctor, see if he needs them.'

'To the physician, you mean? Good idea. We'll be needing them soon,' he said.

Tomorrow.

'Yes,' I said.

'The Norsemen are after our land, and our king. But we're not giving up either of them without a fight.' He smiled, and the lines and furrows in his face deepened, giving him the look of a crumpled-up paper bag.

'Where is the king now?' I asked.

My companion pointed with a dirty forefinger at the bower.

'In there,' he said.

With Aesc, I supposed. I wondered again where Merwenna was.

'Do you know someone called Leofric? One of the thanes?' I asked.

He didn't, but then I saw him.

He was coming through the Great Hall doors, scanning the crowd as if looking for someone, and then clocking me, and waving.

'It *is* you! Wuffa said you were here. God in heaven, I'm glad to see you again, Joss.'

He picked his way through the warriors and all their gear on the floor to get to where I was.

'I thought you'd been cut to pieces by those scumbags,' he said. 'Thank God you weren't. But where've you *been*?'

His face was one bright smile. I was so glad to see him that I smiled back, happiness breaking through me like the sun coming from behind clouds.

'Don't ask me that. I won't be able to tell you,' I said.

He flung his arm round my shoulder, like an old friend.

'I won't ask, then. Come on, let's go and find Merwenna. She'll be so glad you're here.'

Merwenna. The sound of her name, those three little descending syllables, marks made in the dust with a stick, and the thought of her being glad to see me filled me with a fierce joy. I felt my face grow hot. I almost couldn't believe I was going to see her again.

'Yeah, let's. Only I need to give these bits to the physician first. I've forgotten his name.'

'You mean Aethelred,' Leofric said, 'I'll take you. Come on.'

I think the physician remembered me from the time Godfrey had been having his asthma attack. He regarded me with suspicion and dislike when I emptied the coloured packets out of my satchel into his lap.

'What is this trickery?'

'It's not trickery,' Leofric said, 'these are medicines, proper medicines that really work.'

He sounded as earnest and sure as if he knew it – knew it himself I mean, not just because I'd told him and he'd believed me.

I sorted the neat, bright boxes into separate piles. 'Look, these ones are for pain. And these are for preventing infection – wound infections. It's what people use in…in Gipeswic. Very useful after battles.'

I couldn't tell whether Aethelred believed me or not, but if I'd had to guess, I'd say not.

'All right. Now let's go and collect a spear and shield for you. There're spare ones piled up outside the Great Hall,' Leofric said, 'and then we'll find Merwenna. We've got something to tell you too.'

The thought of seeing Merwenna had been so overwhelming that I seemed to have forgotten how to breathe properly, and I felt slightly dizzy. My heart was beating against my ribs like a hammer.

She was so perfectly familiar. When she spoke, her voice was so perfectly her own and no one else's. A bright, glad feeling washed over me, a buzzing like the popping you get in your mouth from eating Space Dust when you're a kid. I was just so happy to see her again after all those centuries apart. When I saw that fair, clear skin, the dusting of freckles across her nose and forehead, I felt in a strange way like I'd come home.

I held her in my arms in a brief hug.

The shape of her inside her clothes made my stomach turn over with longing.

'Joss, we've got a secret to tell you.'

She took my hand and led me behind the wooden fence that enclosed the skinny brown pigs. It was properly morning now and beginning to lightly sleet.

'If you tell me, it won't be a secret any more,' I said.

The spear and shield were much heavier than they looked. I had to lean them on the edge of the pigsty.

'I don't want it to be a secret. I want everyone to know. They will soon anyway.'

Leofric slipped an arm around her shoulder. With a gentle gesture that winded me for a second, he used his forefinger to sweep some sleet-wet hair out of her eyes.

'We are going to be married. This afternoon, in front of

King Edmund,' he said.

'Oh…congratulations,' I said. Then I saw they didn't know what this meant – it must have been another of those words that hadn't been invented yet – so I said, 'I'm really happy for you. For you both.'

Merwenna pushed her arm right through mine, because the mud underfoot was slippery and difficult to balance on.

'Slippery! Hold me up, you two.'

I closed my eyes for a second, but I could still see her behind my squeezed eyelids, happier and more beautiful and joyful than I had ever seen her before. Or seen anyone before.

'If I'm going to die, I want to die your wife,' she said.

'Of course you're not going to die. Nothing bad is going to happen to you,' Leofric said, and kissed her.

The day dragged on and on: the nineteenth day of November. Everyone was hanging about, waiting. All the animals had been moved inside the village enclosure, so they were roaming around, getting under your feet, making a noise and a mess, and you had to be careful of where you stood.

The thanes and other warriors sat in groups around the campfires. There was no more practising in the fields round about. I suppose it felt too late now, when an army of Vikings could be sighted at any moment. Only I knew it would be tomorrow. *Vikings:* it was only me who called them that. To everyone else, they were the Norsemen, or the Danes.

'Why do some of the thanes have armour, and others not?' I asked.

Leofric looked where I was looking: a group of about thirty men wearing thick, padded leather jackets and domed helmets with a tough projecting spur to protect the nose.

'They're the husceorls,' he said. 'Special troops. They belong to King Edmund; they're part of his household. The rest of us have to rely on luck a bit more! But we can find you a helmet, I expect.'

'Are you nervous?' I asked. I didn't know whether I meant the battle, or getting married that afternoon. Both, really.

'No. There's no point in being nervous. What happens, happens,' he said.

☉☉

It happened: they were married in the late afternoon in the Great Hall, by King Edmund of East Anglia. It was the first wedding I had ever been to.

The congregation, if that's the right word for two hundred people wedged shoulder to shoulder in a mass, was as tense as runners on the starting blocks, and half of it was armed to the teeth. Sleet was still coming down outside, the floor rushes had turned to sludge, and damp dogs nosed their way past your legs. But it was also beautiful.

A fire had been lit at each end of the hall, so the room was warm and the walls covered with weirdly dancing orangey shadows. It felt cosy, with the sleety rain drumming outside. And Leofric and Merwenna, standing in front of Edmund, looked beautiful anyway. It was like that thing at school when the golden boy – head boy, captain of the football team, A grades guaranteed – and his girlfriend are somehow godlike compared to the others. Like Rufus Palmier-Thompson and Alice. It's like they're bathed in a special light, like they're bigger and brighter and better than anyone else.

Merwenna and Leofric made me think of a couple of angels, standing there in the firelight while Edmund murmured and then pronounced them man and wife.

Something about Merwenna's bent head made me want to cry. I stopped looking, and concentrated instead on my own hands, clenching the shield Leofric had given me so hard that my knuckles went white with the strain. *Married*. I couldn't get my head around the idea. I hardly knew anyone who was married.

Penda was beside me. His face was one big smile.

'Bravely done,' he said. 'Nothing can part them now, not the Norsemen, nothing.'

I attempted a smile, and made a noise that could have signified agreement, or could have meant I was about to cough, or be sick – anything, really. Penda didn't notice though; he was too busy gazing at Leofric and Merwenna with a fond, soppy look which I suppose people get at weddings.

Edmund held up one hand, and the murmuring swell of whispers died away.

I had met well-known and famous people before; once, our local MP, who was also in the cabinet, came to the dump-school to open the new technology block. And when I was younger, I used to ask footballers for their autographs. And it was always the same. You expect it to be special somehow and it's strange and disappointing when you feel nothing at all when you speak to them and they speak to you; nothing apart from a sort of curiosity that you've seen them on the television and now here they are in the flesh. It's disappointing that they are just people like you and me.

But it didn't feel like that listening to Edmund. You could feel the separateness and difference of him. He wasn't imposing physically; he was a small, slight man with pale skin and large dark eyes, and an unexpected accent which I identified after a second or two as French. I'd imagined robes and jewels and maybe a crown, but this was just a youngish man, pale with tiredness, wearing the same clothes as all the other thanes. There was nothing rich or opulent-looking about him.

But when he spoke, you realised he had something.

He was talking, with a kind of quiet pride, about the coming battle. No, not pride. Conviction – that was it. He had this absolute conviction that it was the right thing to do, and he convinced me of the rightness too. He sounded almost joyful, and some of the joy infected me as well – me, who knew that the battle would be tomorrow, and that we would lose it. 'Bloodbath', Julian had said. But the joy continued – a quite separate feeling.

Edmund said that to fight for what was right, even if you lose, is a kind of victory. And with a sudden shock I thought, he knows he's going to die. He know it as well as I do, but it doesn't make any difference.

'They want to take our land away from us by force. They want to force us to believe in the same gods they believe in. And if we die defending our lands and our faith, then it will be a victorious death.'

You could tell from the nodding and murmurings and general air of the place that everyone in the hall agreed with him. *I* agreed with him, even though I was never the kind of person who gets carried away by speeches or rhetoric. And it wasn't even my fight. But when Edmund spoke, you saw the rightness. He was just that kind of person.

There was such an air of belief in the hall that you could almost see it. Like when Mr Finch, a really inspirational coach – even though he was a dick most of the time – was giving the team talk. By the time he'd finished, all of us really believed we could go out there onto the lumpy pitch behind the Ipswich dump-school and beat Barcelona, if we put our minds to it. The passion of Mr Finch, in his stained, sweaty track suit, was like an injection of belief straight into your heart.

Unfortunately, though, whatever Mr Finch wanted us to believe, it isn't true.

@@

CDAPTER FOURTEEN

❧

weorð myndum
mind's worth (literal translation)

HONOUR

❧

After the wedding, Haegelisdun was tense as hell for the whole day; a lot of milling around, people unable to relax. But not everyone – I saw Wuffa with some of the other thanes sitting around one of the campfires, cradling their weapons in their hands, and they seemed chilled enough. Or maybe it was only on the outside. But most people were fidgety and buzzing. It began to drive me mad. I would almost have welcomed a horde of pillaging Vikings in winged helmets. Anything to end the waiting.

Towards the end of the afternoon I couldn't stand it any more. The sleet had stopped – you could see a square of blue, bitter sky through the wind-eye – so I went outside for some fresh air. Fresh air, hah! The air wasn't just fresh, it was so clear and searing cold that it hurt your lungs to breathe in. But the deathly cold was better than being crushed in the hall.

They had sealed shut the gates in the wooden perimeter wall, but there was a place next to the dyeing house where you could slip through easily enough if you were thin like I was.

I felt so much better once I was through that I played with the idea of just walking and walking; away from all the strangeness and twitchy tension of Haegelisdun; walking and ending up I didn't know where – back in Ipswich maybe. Or the other way, towards the sea. The whale road, Merwenna called it.

All of a sudden, it was a beautiful evening. The steely blue sky was dotted with small, puffy purple clouds which looked unreal, as if they been painted on afterwards. The row of trees on the ridge in front of me made black spiky patterns against the sky, which, low-down on the horizon, was no longer blue but a vivid orangey pink. The line between blue and pink was just above the tops of the trees, and straight, as if someone had drawn it there with a ruler. And hanging in the thin air was a single white star.

I recognised Merwenna when she was still a hundred metres away. She was walking quickly up the hill, and there were two of the hairy, wolf-shaped dogs bounding around her, nose down in the undergrowth and carrying their plumy tails like flagpoles.

'Merwenna! Wait for me, I'll catch you up.'

She turned and waved, and waited till I had scrambled up to her.

'Joss! You're not really supposed to be out. Neither am I,' she said.

'Why *are* you?' I asked. I was trying to hide how out of breath I was.

'Oh, I don't know exactly. The rain stopped, and I couldn't bear being cooped up like that any more. And because I was so happy, I couldn't keep still. Do you know what I mean?'

'Where's Leofric?' I asked.

'He's on watch patrol tonight.' She waved her arm vaguely, indicating where. 'The other side of the ridge. Looking out for Vikings,' she said.

'But it's your wedding night,' I said.

The words 'wedding night' sounded full of lumps when I said it, like a phrase I'd learnt from a book, nothing to do with me.

Merwenna laughed. 'There'll be other nights, lots of other nights. If we're lucky,' she said.

I said nothing. There might not be other nights; we both knew that. This time tomorrow, we would probably all be dead. Life was so temporary.

How strange that I'd never given it a thought before, in Ipswich, I mean. You'd go out to work or to the shops or to school, just doing normal stuff every day, and you never even thought how it might all be over any minute. Like blowing out a candle. The line between life and death was such a fine one, fragile as the walls of a bubble, and yet we thought we were so clever, with our warm houses and our penicillin and cars and phones and endless electric light. But it could all be gone in an instant.

I swallowed hard.

'I'm glad you're happy,' I said.

'And I'm glad you're back. From wherever you'd been all that time.'

We walked down the path side by side, hands by our sides, not quite touching.

'I went home,' I said. Not true, but near enough.

'Sometimes I think…you're so mysterious, Joss. You know so much more than we do. Leofric told me about the medicines you gave to Aethelred. Sometimes I think you're from a different world. Cleverer.'

'It's the same world,' I said. 'Even on the other side of the whale road, it's still the same world. And believe me, it's no cleverer, that's for sure.'

She pulled her shawl closer around her shoulders. I had forgotten how cold it was, but now I realised my hands had gone blue, and my bones felt like they might snap with it.

'We ought to go back, I suppose,' I said.

'In a minute. It's so pretty out here now it's stopped raining. Look at the sky over there, Joss! It's so pretty, it hurts. Do you know what I mean?'

I did; so completely that for a second I felt quite winded. I knew exactly what she meant – that curious, hungry pain you get when you look at something beautiful.

I'd thought it was some peculiar quirk of my own.

When I kissed Alice it had been, if not exactly planned in advance, at least something we'd both known would happen. It was just a question of when.

But I didn't know I was kissing Merwenna until it was happening. Her skin and lips were soft and dry and very cold. Brave and uncomplaining, fleetingly lovely Merwenna, pressed against me for one moment of cold and darkening sky.

She pulled away, but without any of the meaningless huffing and puffing and pretend outrage I associate with girls. Her face was as smooth and calm as it always was. Winter glittered in her hair, and she pulled her scarf closer, throwing the ends over her shoulder in a gesture I realised I knew from somewhere.

'I'm going back,' she said.

'All right.'

I watched her as she and the two dogs went back down the hill, and through the gap in the wall into Haegelisdun, and then I walked aimlessly on. I walked until it got dark, and then I went back as well.

I didn't see her again that evening. I'd gone back to the Great Hall and had some more soup from the pot, then after a couple of hours in the stewed and used-up air I needed to go outside again. It had started to rain again – a thin, slanting rain that hurt when it hit your face – but it was better than another minute of that sour smell.

The smell, the cold, the stink and repellent squelch of the toilet pits, the painful winter cold – I'd never thought about it before, but this was what history really meant. Noise and smells and cold. And sunsets and laughing till you choked, and the feel of a girl in your arms. Not someone like Mr Richards in a mid-price suit standing in front of you yakking on about the spinning jenny or the railways or the Year of Revolutions. There might be moments of glory and importance, but they were few and far between. Mostly, history was long spells of time being cramped and uncomfortable and cold. But the man in the suit at the front of the classroom only wants to remember the important bits, and the glorious battles.

I needed to speak to King Edmund about a glorious battle, the one we would be having tomorrow.

He was inside one of the huts near the Great Hall, surrounded by about twenty of the husceorls. I could just see him, sitting on a chair by the fire in the middle of the room. They went everywhere with him – the husceorls, I mean – even when he went to the toilet pits, which personally I would have found unnerving.

Wiping the icy rain off my face, I went towards Edmund, but before I'd got within a few metres of him, there were three men barring my way, their swords drawn and pointed at my head.

'Who wants to see the king?'

The speaker was the closest guard to me, and he seemed about two metres tall from where I was standing, towering over me in the light of a wall torch that made his helmet and shield glint and flash.

'My name's Joss. I'm a stranger, from…from Gipeswic.'
I tried to twist around to catch King Edmund's eye, but it
was hard because the guard had my neck in a grip. 'I need
to speak to you, Edmund, sir.'

I think it was the first time in my life I had ever called
anyone 'sir', but it wasn't servile enough for the husceorls,
who called me a filthy dog, offered to cut my throat for me
and seemed to want me to conduct my conversation with
Edmund on my hands and knees with my face pressed
against the sludgy rushes on the floor.

'Wait, Redwald. Joss is a newcomer; his ways are bound
to be different to ours. It doesn't mean they're wrong.'

Redwald looked unconvinced. He was still holding onto
me, at the tender bit where your neck joins your shoulder,
harder than he needed to and it hurt.

'Peace, Redwald.'

I jerked my head free.

Arsehole.

Edmund beckoned me closer.

What did you say to kings? Oh, yes, that was it: 'Your
Majesty, I've got something to tell you. Something private,
for your ears only. Can I talk to you alone, I mean?'

Edmund smiled as if I'd said something funny. Perhaps
'Your Majesty' had been wrong.

It might only have been a trick of the firelight, but he
looked very pale, and there was a nimbus of dark stubble
outlining his cheeks and chin. Up close, I noticed that his
heavy eyelids and thick, dark lashes gave him the look,

somehow, of a baby animal.

'I don't have any secrets from my husceorls,' he said. 'Whatever you want to say to me, you can say to them as well.'

This was awkward.

I took a deep breath and told him about how the battle was going to be a bloodbath, and that we would lose, and he would be tied to a tree and shot full of arrows.

I could see they all thought I was mad.

I sounded mad, even to myself – hot and stumbling and incoherent. And what would I say if they asked me how I knew all this? Oh, God, I'd have to say I'd had a vision or something and that would make me feel ridiculous, a New Age-y loser who believes in any old crap, like the kind of person Tracy was friends with – people I'd always despised. And I didn't know what they did to witches or people who predicted the future. I might be burnt at the stake or drowned in the river or something.

The thing was, Edmund didn't seem interested in why I thought I knew what was going to happen. He didn't even seem bothered by the apocalyptic vision of death and destruction I'd described. In fact, it seemed to give him a bit of kick, if I'm honest. A rapt, determined light shone out of his eyes.

'If I am to die, I will die in the name of Christ,' he said.

He said it gravely, like he was expecting it to be written down for posterity. Like he knew exactly how much of a pithy, powerful soundbite it was, and wanted everyone else to notice it too.

I felt myself growing irritated.

Because it was all very well, all this noble talk of dying in the name of Christ. It sounded admirable and important – Dying In The Name of Christ – only the reality was going to be very different. The reality was pain and fear and your cheek in the mud and your blood spilling out all over the place. Dying was dying, however you dressed it up. There had to be a better way of getting your point across. I remembered Julian saying something similar that afternoon when we were drinking lemonade on the scratchy, parched yellow lawn in Cressida and Tim's garden. There was nothing new about killing, and dying. I was suddenly homesick for all that: for Julian and Hoxne, for electric lights and radiators and seatbelts in cars, for all the ordinary things that kept you safe and warm because you mattered and so did your life. I wanted to feel safe again.

I didn't say anything, but my irritation must have showed in my face because Edmund said, gently, 'Joss. Don't be so fearful. We've all got to die some day, haven't we?'

'I'm not fearful—' I began, but he cut me off.

'So if I die tomorrow, or in ten years' time, what difference does it make?'

'It might make a difference to someone,' I said.

We were getting away from the point, which was that unless something changed, tomorrow's bloodbath would be fatal for him and probably for me as well, and for pretty much everyone else.

'Not a real difference. The sun would still come up in

the morning just the same. And to die for something you believe in with all your heart – isn't that better than dying falling off a horse or catching an ague or getting a growth in the guts? Or even dying at the point of a heathen sword, defending your land. Do you understand what I mean?'

'Sort of,' I said.

I did, sort of, but it wasn't what I wanted to hear. What I wanted to hear was that Edmund accepted completely what I'd told him, and that tomorrow's battle would be avoided or postponed indefinitely, if he couldn't work out a way to win it. But Edmund seemed to find the battle almost irrelevant, a side issue, compared to the importance of dying a martyr's death.

They all saw it differently, I realised.

Wuffa, and probably Leofric, were brave and uncompromising – this was their land, and if anyone wanted it they were going to have to come and take if off them. They were going to fight to the last drop of their blood and the last drop of everyone else's. I'd hated Wuffa when I first met him, probably because he had scared the shit out of me, but I'd always known that about him. Brave and loyal and uncompromising. And Aesc, who was just as brave but more of a realist. He was probably right when he said the Vikings wouldn't want wholesale slaughter necessarily, that they'd need people alive at the end to work the land and tend the animals. His idea that negotiation might be possible had angered Wuffa, but that didn't make it wrong. And then there were the foot soldiers, people like Penda, who would do what they were told without thinking or having a debate about it.

I didn't think I'd realised until now how many different ways there were of looking at the same thing.

They were all, I thought, equally right and equally wrong.

'Don't worry,' Edmund said, 'it was good of you to let me know your thoughts. But I'm prepared for what's to come. God grant you a good night.'

I realised I was being dismissed.

'OK. Goodnight, then,' I said.

I turned to go, and one of the husceorls, the one called Redwald, aimed a vicious kick at my shins.

'You don't turn your back on the king, you little piece of shit. Where are your manners? Back out and bend your bloody knee or I'll bend it for you.'

I wanted to snarl something back at him: don't talk to me like that, and don't you bloody kick me. But it was late, and I was tired and also, suddenly, overwhelmed. I had kissed Merwenna, who was not mine to kiss, and tomorrow I would die in a battle I no longer had the slightest conviction I would be able to influence. I backed out of the hut, and into the foggy, freezing dark.

The campfires were blurred orange glows in the fog, as if behind smoked glass. You could see the lumpy shapes of a few people hanging over them to keep warm, but most people were squeezed inside the stinking huts, and I, for one, didn't blame them. It was cold and getting colder, and my footsteps were starting to crunch on the ice forming on the muddy ground.

I should go in, I thought. I headed in the direction of the Great Hall, but three steps later I collided with someone, someone sturdy and wide and shapeless in the fog under layers of woollen shawls and thick, prickly blankets.

'Joss, is that you? I've been looking all over. I heard you were back.'

'Cyneburga…hello. Yeah, I'm back. How…how are you?' I couldn't keep the gladness out of my voice. I wasn't faking it, I really was glad to see her again. I wanted to say more, but speeches were never my thing and anyway she had given my arm a little shake, like a terrier with a rat, and then she was towing me through the gloom like a wheeled suitcase through Arrivals.

'I've got something for you. Wait here,' she said.

She went into one of the houses – her own, I guessed, although in the fog it was unrecognisable – and came out in a minute or two.

'Can't swing a cat in there. Half the rabble of East Anglia's in Haegelisdun. And my house smells like the inside of a soldier's boot,' she said.

'Nice to have the company, though,' I said. I really felt at that moment like I loved the crotchety woman. Her constant grumbling about everything was background noise, I had come to realise, masking but not drowning out the compelling need in her to look after everyone who stepped into the Eadwig-shaped space in her life.

'Here,' she said, and pushed some heavy, unwieldy objects into my arms. I couldn't really see much in the darkness, but when I felt them, I knew what they were.

'I've polished Eadwig's helmet for you. And that's his old spear. And here's his shield. I was worried you wouldn't have anything to protect you,' she said.

'Oh, Cyneburga. Leofric found me a shield, but it's pretty knackered. This is much better. Thank you,' I said.

She made a huffing, snorting sort of sound.

'You can give them back when it's all over. All this foolishness. God's on our side, though, not those heathens from God in heaven knows where. You'll see.'

I felt suddenly as if I wanted to hug her.

'Yeah, well. I hope you're right, Cyneburga,' I said.

I didn't expect to sleep, but in fact I fell asleep at once, crushed between a couple of armed men and the wall of the Great Hall. I woke up before the dawn, abruptly and suddenly as if someone had shouted my name.

The fire was almost out. There was a thin sheen of frost on the blanket I'd pulled over me, and my breath hung in the air like smoke.

I'd forgotten how horrible it felt, waking up in your clothes. I uncurled, and picked my way outside. I was wearing Eadwig's helmet, to save carrying it, and the broad projecting band pressed against my nose and chafed it. I hooked the shield over my arm, and held the spear upright, like a flag.

Outside, the air was bone-cold and tasted of ice. The bleached grey light of early morning made everything look washed out, but at least the fog had gone. It was my second Haegelisdun dawn in two days.

People were just beginning to stir. Women, mainly, getting the fires started and chopping and chucking stuff into the hanging pots to cook for breakfast. I looked for Merwenna, but she wasn't there.

And then there was a noise behind me, a noise I didn't recognise for a beat or two but then I did: horses' hooves. And then the locked gate was opening and three riders on horseback came in; the scouts were back, and one of them had long, fair hair under the domed helmet. Leofric. There was suddenly shouting and movement and urgency, and people pouring out of the houses and running about in a chaos of noise and panicky action.

Like an anthill, I thought, when you stir it with a stick.

'The Norsemen...the Norsemen are coming!'

The panic and shouting seemed to have very little to do with me. It was as if I was a long way off, watching it all from a distant star.

Someone caught my arm and jerked me out of my stillness.

'Joss! Don't stand there dreaming.'

It was Leofric. He'd slipped from the back of the horse he'd been riding, and it was skittering around in all the confusion, the whites of its eyes showing, till someone caught the bridle and dragged it off.

'Norsemen. About three miles away. Go and find one of the thanes, Joss, they'll tell you what to do,' he shouted.

I came out of my reverie, and noticed in the interested,

detached way you notice things that aren't important, that my hands were shaking, doing a mad crab-dance of their own.

'God, Leofric, I'm sorry. I wanted it to be different, but I fucked up. I'm sorry,' I said.

I didn't think with all the noise around us he had heard me, and anyway he wasn't listening.

He pulled me towards him, looking at me very intensely as if he was going to say something of enormous significance, only he didn't speak at all.

We were staring at each other, a freeze-frame in the motionless eye of the storm around us.

'I'm sorry, Leofric. I'm sorry,' I said.

'I'm sorry' was the only phrase that formed itself in my brain.

'Joss, listen to me. I want to ask you something. If I die today and you don't…listen to me, it's important…if you don't, then promise me. Promise me you'll look after Merwenna. I love her so much.'

I felt sick with the knowledge of how badly I'd let him down.

'Yes, of course I will. Of course I will. I promise,' I said.

He nodded and let go of my arm.

'Good. Thank you. And now it's time to go,' he said.

☉☉

ChAPTER FIFTEEN

❦

hilde scur
battle shower (literal translation)

FLIGHT OF ARROWS

❦

Time to go. I am swept with the rest of the village out of the gates. Confusion and shouting, no one seems to know what to do. Somehow we are arranged in lines; I am in the second row. I don't know how many rows there are behind me, but I sense a lot. I don't know how many of us there are. I don't know anything. I can't see any faces I recognise. Everyone I might have known is transformed by helmets and spears into violent strangers. Leofric said they were three miles away. Where is Leofric?

The Anglo-Saxon army is moving, and I am moving with it, helpless as a twig in a stream. Uphill, then down. We stop. It is light now, the sun is up. When did that happen? I grip Eadwig's spear, hold his shield against my chest like the others are doing. I am trying to feel like a soldier.

I know this place. It's the fishing place, the bit of the river where Leofric set up his lines. Last time I was here it had been shimmering with heat and dragonflies and the hot, soapy smell of things growing. Now it's just mud – thick, sticky mud, and dead, brown reedy stuff stiffened with the cold. It's so wet and slippery underfoot it's going to be like fighting on an ice rink. Some big birds take off from the trees by the river and flap noisily away. We have frightened them.

I am frightened.

The world is yellow and brown, apart from the sky, which is a dirty white. Someone is muttering a prayer behind me. I am not the only one who is frightened. A smaller bird lands on a wet branch in front of us. I watch it watching us with its treacle-black eyes and wonder why I have never noticed before what a miracle of delicate engineering birds are: the hinged legs; the cruel, tiny beak; the hollow bones that weigh nothing at all. I have wasted so much time not noticing things and now, suddenly, there is no time left.

A murmur, a crackle of electricity running through us. They're here; the Norsemen are here. I can see them in the gap between the men in front of me. They're on the other side of the river, lined up like we are, only I think there're more of them. Lots more – maybe twice as many. They're lined up in a V shape, I see now, not in rows like us. They don't have wings on their helmets. History must have made that up, a pleasing picturesque detail but not, as Julian might say, fundamentally true. They are shouting and taunting us. I can't understand the words, but the meaning is pretty clear. And the husceorls behind me and to my left start the response. Which stutters a bit at first, then everyone is shouting and taunting back.

We can't hear them properly and they can't hear us properly but the shouting carries on for quite a while. It reminds me of the jeers and chanting you get at football matches.

Then the noise dies down, and at a sharp cry from behind me everyone around me puts their shield up above their head, like you hold a newspaper to save your hair getting wet in the rain, so I do it too, only it isn't rain but arrows that are coming down hard on us. One hits Eadwig's shield and it's so hard it makes my whole body jolt with the force of it. One hits the man next to me, skewering him through his shoulder and spiking him to the ground. He makes a grunting noise, then nothing. His eyes are open, and fixed on nothing. There is only a very little blood, collecting round the shaft of the arrow like the petals of a flower. He is the first dead person I have ever seen.

Anglo-Saxon archers behind me are firing back at the Vikings. The space above my shielded head is thick with arrows. How will I know what to do? I can't see I can't see I can't see.

But then the arrows stop, and everyone comes out from under their shields. I can see that on the other side of the river, the Viking army has formed itself more tightly into the V shape, and is coming closer, not charging but moving steadily and purposefully at a pace somewhere between a walk and a quick trot. My insides shrivel in fear as I watch them entering the river as if it isn't there, coming closer and closer. Archers from somewhere behind me start firing arrows at them again, and some of the Viking soldiers fall in the water, but not enough; not enough.

I think 'Merwenna', and picture her, waiting behind the locked village gates, and it's the last coherent thought I have because then they've reached us and then it's just confusion: metal noise, of weapons hitting other weapons and clashing against shields and helmets; human noise of men shouting and horrible screams of pain. The noise is all around me but it's too much for my brain to process, and nothing makes sense. I am struggling simply to stay on my feet.

The Vikings are better armed than we are. They have long, heavy axes which they slash from side to side like people cutting hay. They can take a man's head from his shoulders, and the reason I know this is because I see it happen: a vicious swing catches a man in my eyeline under his chin and suddenly half his face is missing and there is only a bloody mess. I can't think straight. There is only pain and noise and chaos. Everything is blurred with occasional flashes of clarity. I see a man getting a blow in his throat from a sword and the next second he is suddenly and dramatically drenched in blood – really drenched I mean, as if someone has hosed him down with red paint. I see an arm on its own, sliced off and flying through the air.

I see someone clutching the place where their belly used to be, only it's just blood and mush there now.

Someone is leaning heavily against me and I heave him off. He falls and lies backward in the mud with his eyes open and frozen blue and fixed on the sky. There is no room in my head for anything other than the awful noise, the bodies, the shields that keep banging into me and knocking the breath out of me. All the time I'm flailing with Eadwig's short spear and round shield, not fighting but simply trying to stay upright and not fall. If I fell I'd have no chance. I'd be crushed in the mud and trampled to death by hundreds of heedless feet. I swing Eadwig's shield, dodging what I can but basically helpless, a bit of rubbish buffeted about in a rough sea.

I don't know how long it goes on for.

But then suddenly it's over and we have lost. There's no signal or anything to tell us, but the knowledge that we are finished spreads through what's left of the Anglo-Saxons like wind rippling through a field of corn. We are being beaten back, back towards the settlement. The sky is blank and undisturbed above the slaughter.

I turn and run with the others. I'm not aware of much any more but my own fear and confusion, but I can see there aren't many of us left, and that the Vikings are just behind us, roaring their triumph and waving those heavy axes from side to side. My brain registers Wuffa beside me, his face and chest covered in blood. And then suddenly he isn't there any more. He's tripped over a root or something, and is sprawled on the ground, with one of the pursuing

Vikings poised, arm up, ready to finish him off as he lies there. I skid to a stop and throw myself against the attacker, with no particular plan or aim, but the rim of Eadwig's shield catches the Viking under the chin and the point of Eadwig's spear jabs into his exposed throat and suddenly there is blood everywhere, like a fountain, and then Wuffa is scrambling up.

'Come on. Come on!'

My legs are numb and soft with the horror of it. I've killed someone. I've killed someone. I didn't mean to, but I've killed someone, and by doing it I have saved Wuffa from death. I have gone numb and stupid with the shock of it.

'Come on, Joss, move!'

Wuffa drags me with him, and we get through the gates of Haegelisdun just before they are hastily shut and bolted behind us.

Wuffa let go of me, and I went spinning away into the chaos and noise. You could hear women screaming now, adding to the clamour, and there was a strong and sudden smell of smoke. I ran, basically because there was nothing else I could do; I ran and ran until my breath was coming in great, tearing gasps. Any moment now and asthma would grip me, a fist closing on two empty paper bags.

Behind me the gates fell in with a cracking, splintering sound, and the noise and screaming surged up a notch, like a football game when someone scores a goal.

I was emptied out with fear and exhaustion. I couldn't run any further. I'd got as far as the edge of the village, where most of the pigs and cows were kept; the smoke and noise had unsettled them and their eyes were wide and foolish with fear. But the rest of nature was unconcerned. The brown river was glassy and calm, reflecting the sky and the leafless trees and the wooden bridge. Nature doesn't care, I realised. The sun was even trying to come out.

I crouched down and leant forward, trying to drag some air into my lungs. Breathe, breathe. I could see a few other people who'd run this far, but like me, they were finished. We had no more fight in us, any of us; we were just waiting for the end.

I sank to a sitting position with my back against the pigsty. I closed my eyes and waited for the next thing to happen. Time passed, but I couldn't say how long. I think I may even have fallen into a sort of dazed half-sleep.

And then I heard stumbling footsteps behind me followed by a heavy crash and jolt as two men staggered around the corner of the sty and collapsed against me.

Anglo-Saxons, was my first thought.

Edmund, was my second.

He was gasping for breath and I could see his arms were shaking as if from some huge effort.

'Help me,' he said, 'he's badly injured…I've had to almost carry him from the village.'

Both Edmund and the man he was supporting were extravagantly covered in blood.

'Edmund…are you all right?' I asked.

'I'm all right. Not even a scratch…but this man's badly hurt. He took a spear in his side to protect me – he saved my life.'

'He's still alive,' I said. I took off his helmet and wiped the blood from his face, and then I saw it was Wuffa.

His skin was grey, and he was hardly breathing. I could tell without any medical training whatsoever that he was about to die.

'My husceorls are all dead. This man saved me from joining them,' Edmund said. He squatted on the muddy ground, supporting Wuffa's head on his knees. 'Do you know him?'

'Yes, it's Wuffa. Oh, God,' I said, 'I haven't even got that bloody morphine.'

Even in the middle of all the chaos and fear, the knowledge of a battle lost and God knows what to come, there was room in me for anguish. I was amazed, because Wuffa was an unpleasant, brutal, violent bully, but he wasn't only that, and I was in anguish watching him die. If only there was something I could do.

Wuffa's eyes opened without any demure fluttering and he looked straight at me. It was impossible to tell if he recognised me.

'Look after the king,' he said.

'I will. Wuffa, hang on in there. I'm going to try and stop the bleeding,' I said.

'Don't bother,' Wuffa said. His voice had shrunk almost to a whisper, and you could see how much effort every word was taking. 'Don't trouble. I die happy, knowing the king is safe.'

I started to feel for an opening in his tunic, to try and locate where the blood was coming from, but it was too late. I hadn't even found the wound when his eyes glazed and I could feel the life draining out of his body, leaving it slack and heavy like a sack of old stones.

I laid his head gently down on the ground.

'Oh, God. Poor Wuffa.'

Poor all of us. I wondered what had happened to Leofric and Aesc. And Merwenna. I didn't want to think about her and what might have happened to her, because it was just too painful to contemplate, even for a second.

And then I realised something. I realised that if Wuffa had taken a spear in the side to protect Edmund, then in a way it was my doing because ten minutes earlier, almost accidentally, I had saved Wuffa from a Viking sword. If I hadn't done what I did, King Edmund would be dead now. I'd saved Wuffa, and so I had also saved Edmund. I had done it. I had done what I'd come back for. I'd made a difference.

The smoke was getting thicker, and my eyes were stinging with it. I looked across the pigsty, back at the village, and I could see that about half the houses, including the Great Hall, were burning. The Vikings must have decided they were going to burn Haegelisdun to the ground.

There was no more fighting, but the ground in the village was scattered with bodies. And I could hear the sound of voices, though not what they were saying. Hard, jeering voices.

'They're coming this way. We need to get out of here,' I said.

Looking back towards Haegelisdun, I could see that every Anglo-Saxon who was still alive had been corralled into one group at the edge of the village, and you could see six or seven Viking soldiers standing with them, their swords held high like javelins pointing at them. The stragglers were being picked off one by one, dragged into the corral or just cut down, depending on how much fight they put up.

'We've got to go. Come on, Edmund. Quick!' I said.

His eyes were closed, and his lips were moving gently. He was praying, I realised.

'Not now, for God's sake,' I said, 'they're coming this way and it's you they're looking for. Quick, come with me!'

I took him by the arm and dragged him with me. If we ran, we might be able to get across the field and up the hill; we could cross the ridge and hide in the trees.

But they were too close. We'd never make it – the ridge was just too far.

I slipped in the mud at the side of the river. The clamour and voices behind us were nearer and clearer.

'We'll have to hide. Under the bridge, Edmund. Move!' I said.

You know the ending. I knew the ending, but I was still determined it wouldn't end like that. I'd saved Edmund, or at least I'd saved Wuffa, which amounted to the same thing in the end. I was determined, if it was the last bloody thing

I did, to prevent Edmund being found under the bridge, dragged out and forced to die his martyr's death, stuck full of the arrows that had rained down on us during the battle – arrows thick as a man's thumb and armed with a barb sharp and vicious as a Stanley knife.

'Don't move. Don't make a sound,' I whispered to Edmund.

I was worried in case he wanted to stride out theatrically to meet his martyr's fate. 'If I am to die, I will die in the name of Christ.' I pushed him behind me, into the shadows under the bridge. You could hear the sound of footsteps coming nearer, the sound of voices, and was that horses? Yes, horses' hooves. I wanted to close my eyes, like dogs do when they don't want you to find them.

The footsteps got nearer. I could hear Viking voices: loud, confident and full of victory. What Tracy would call cocky.

I didn't dare to move, but I sent fierce, concentrated thought-messages to Edmund, at the same time as keeping my back firmly pushed against him, pushing him against the underside of the bridge. Don't move. Don't breathe. Don't cough. Both of us were standing up to our knees in the freezing water, and the cold got right into your bones. I wanted, desperately, to piss.

Don't move.

The victorious Viking army swarmed onto the bridge. The feet and hooves were loud and echoey on the wet wooden planks over our heads. I pulled Edmund down, till we were crouching with only our head and shoulders poking out of the water.

God, it's so cold.

Please don't let them see us.

I felt as big and conspicuous as if I was standing in the middle of the bridge on a soapbox and holding a sign saying 'here I am!'

But miraculously, they didn't see us.

The steady tramp of feet and the clacketing sounds of hooves passed overhead without a break in their rhythm. I let out a long, shaky breath. They hadn't seen us, even though Alice and Julian had both said they would, and that felt significant, as if another tiny corner had been turned.

Only one person spotted us.

Leofric.

He was stumbling, weaponless and bloody, among a load of other thanes and some of the husceorls, all of them battered and obviously prisoners of war. They were being herded, like cattle, towards the edge of Haegelisdun, and their heads were bowed in defeat, whilst the ones doing the herding were laughing and shouting to each other and looked like they were having the time of their lives.

Some instinct, I don't know what, must have told Leofric to glance up precisely when he did, just before he stepped onto the wooden planks of the bridge. He was horribly injured, his helmet had gone and you could see his fair hair was caked in brown blood. He looked blank and exhausted, wiped out by what had happened, and he was holding one arm awkwardly, at an angle, as if it hurt him. And the other arm, I saw, suddenly, was around Merwenna.

Oh, God, Merwenna.

Keep still. Don't move.

Leofric lifted his head and looked straight at me for maybe half a second, straight into my eyes, and I knew from the hardly perceptible stiffening of his shoulders that he'd recognised us.

I kept perfectly still, pressing Edmund back to the wall.

The footsteps over the bridge stopped after a while and I waited but there weren't any more. I guessed that was it and risked a quick look out to see what was happening.

The smell of smoke was much stronger, and you could hear the crackle of fires where the huts and houses were burning. Fire is loud. I never knew that before the night in another lifetime when Tracy burnt down our house. It makes a hard, roaring sound that you can't talk over. And the smoke clogs your throat, and makes your eyes swell and water.

The Vikings rounded everyone up in a rough semicircle in front of the animal yards. There wasn't much commotion, only a bit of crying from some of the children. I couldn't see Leofric for a minute, and then there he was: a flash of blond hair, his arm still around Merwenna.

A ragged cheer went up from the Vikings, a loud, male noise, barbed with pride. One of them had climbed up onto a low wall and was making a speech – a victory speech by the look of it, punctuated with fist pumps and more male cheering. Ivar the Boneless. It must be him.

There was a small, splashing sound behind me, and I felt a hand on my arm.

'Get back, Edmund. They mustn't see you,' I said.

I pushed him back. It was imperative he stay hidden. It was suddenly the most important thing I had ever done, or would ever do. I'd been unable to change anything else for the better in my whole life before: Tracy, my dad buggering off before I'd learnt to walk, being shoved into different places by different well-meaning interferers like Sofia. I'd been helpless in the face of all that, helpless and ridiculous as a goldfish struggling on a living-room carpet. But this I could change. I could save Edmund.

'I need to know what's happening.'

'I'll tell you what's happening. Get back,' I said, but he wouldn't. He stood next to me instead, shoulder to shoulder under the bridge, partially obscured by a fallen tree and with the cold brown water soaking into our clothes.

'What's he doing?' I whispered.

'Gloating, maybe,' Edmund whispered back, 'or praying. Praying to their filthy heathen gods.'

But I didn't think Ivar the Boneless was doing either of these. It looked more like someone making a political speech. His voice kept cracking as he raised it, as if his emotions were getting the better of him, and he was driving his fist repeatedly into the palm of his other hand for emphasis.

It reminded me of something. Scratchy old black and white films you see sometimes on TV of Hitler shouting and haranguing before a forest of right arms all held up in the Nazi salute. A thousand years before you had the Third Reich, you already had this.

'He's shouting at them,' I said.

'He's demanding to know where I am,' Edmund said. He spoke with a kind of quiet satisfaction. I held my hand up to shush him and listened intently. He was right. Ivar the Boneless, fists flying all over the place, was ordering what was left of the Anglo-Saxons to give up their king. I strained my ears to hear him better.

'I won't harm him. Not a hair of his head. I'm offering him peace, and a chance to rule jointly with me. Ours will be a partnership. A great and shared partnership for peace.'

'He's lying,' I said.

I can always tell when people are lying. Always. Tracy says it's because I'm such a good liar myself but whatever, I can always tell.

Edmund said, 'I must go to him.'

'You must bloody not,' I said, 'he's lying through his teeth. He'll kill you. You've got to believe me, Edmund, I know he will.'

'I know. But I've got to go. If I die in the name of Christ, it's no death at all.'

I shoved him as hard as I could against the underside of the bridge.

'No! Dead is dead; doesn't matter whose name it's in. The whole reason I'm here is to prevent them killing you.'

'You can't,' Edmund said gently. 'Killing is in their nature. Things are as they are, you can't change them.'

I felt desperate.

'No. You're staying under this bridge until they're gone,' I said.

'How will history judge me if I hide under here like a coward?' he asked. He spoke quietly, but his eyes were burning.

The idea that this *was* history flittered across my mind. I'd read that butterfly book in Year 9, I knew it was dangerous to change the past. But if saving Edmund's life meant that the world would have a different future, then so what? It could hardly be any fucking worse.

'Don't worry about history,' I said bitterly, 'it's all lies anyway.

'Something's happening,' Edmund said.

Ivar the Boneless had stopped shouting and said something to a couple of his men. Who plunged into the little knot of Anglo-Saxons and dragged someone out to stand in front of him.

Leofric.

'Quiet. We need to listen,' I said.

'Where's your king? Where's Edmund? I know you know where he is. Tell me where he is, boy,' Ivar said.

I saw Leofric shake his head. He said something as well, but it was too muffled for me to hear.

One of the Norsemen drove his fist into Leofric's gut. He doubled up, and then the Norseman hit him again, this time in the teeth. I saw blood fly out of his mouth and spatter on the ground.

I felt my hands form themselves into fists.

'Tell me,' Ivar said again.

And then I heard Merwenna.

Her voice rang out, calm as it always was, but assured and

loud enough for us to hear her words without straining. My brave Merwenna. My stomach convulsed with love.

'He doesn't know. And even if he did, I command him to remain silent.'

'Command?' asked Ivar.

'I'm Aesc's daughter. Now that he's dead, I'm in command of these people. And I command him to be silent,' Merwenna said.

Ivar laughed, the horrible pretend laugh people use when they don't think it's funny but want you to think they do. He got off the wall and grabbed her. I saw her stumble as he pulled her to face him, standing apart from the others next to Leofric, and I felt such rage I wanted to spit with it. I could feel myself shaking all over with hatred for Ivar. What gave him the *right*? What gave him the right to do any of this?

'I have to go. I'll go and show them I'm here,' Edmund said.

'No!' I said. It was difficult to argue with him in whispers. You can't sound as serious as you want to sound, if you're whispering.

'You've got to survive this,' I said, 'so you can tell people what really happened. If you don't, it'll be their version that everyone knows.'

History is written by the winners. I was sure I had heard Mr Richards say this.

Edmund opened his mouth, as if he was about to call out.

I clapped my hand over it and struggled to keep it there.

'No, Edmund. Keep quiet, for God's sake.'

Ivar took the doubled-headed axe out of his belt.

'Let's see if he keeps quiet when I'm about to knock your head off your shoulders,' he said.

Two of his heavies caught hold of Leofric, one arm each, so he had no choice but to stand there, stand there and watch helplessly.

Merwenna said calmly, 'He will.'

I stared wildly at Leofric. He had gone white, not merely pale but white like chalk or paper. And his teeth were clenched together tightly. He looked as if he might faint, or be sick or something, at any moment.

'I will do it, you know,' Ivar said. 'One more Saxon head in the mud means nothing to me. Nothing at all.'

Edmund tried again to pull away. I jammed my forearm across his chest, using all my weight to force him back into the shadows under the bridge.

'He won't tell you. None of these people will betray their king. It doesn't matter how many heads you knock off,' Merwenna said.

Both Ivar's hands were gripping the axe handle. He drew it back. Slowly, calmly. This wasn't for show, he really was going to kill her.

Leofric's whole body jolted, like an electric current was going right through it. And suddenly I knew he wasn't going to say anything. He wasn't going to betray Edmund, and me, even if it meant Merwenna was going to die.

Ivar moved the axe slowly towards her, measuring the distance.

Edmund was trying to pull away from me. I still had my hand over his mouth, but it was a fight to keep it there.

Ivar drew back his axe. Leofric looked as though his legs were giving way under him. His face was a mask of pain and horror.

I let go of Edmund.

I let go, because I couldn't bear what they were going to do to Merwenna. I couldn't bear it, which must mean I'm not as strong as Leofric. Or something. I'm not too sure; sometimes when you start to think about people and why they do the things they do, it all gets too complicated for me. People are the way they are, just like Edmund said. He got to be the sacrificial lamb after all, scrambling towards Ivar the Boneless almost joyfully.

They dragged me out from under the bridge, slapped me around a bit, and then shoved me over to stand with the others. It was Edmund they were after, not me. They were so elated about having him in their hands, they didn't bother with me too much.

I was so cold I couldn't feel my legs. My clothes were so heavy with water it was hard to stand up in them. I stumbled, and more or less fell at Merwenna's feet.

She and Leofric picked me up.

'It's all right, Joss. Lean on Leofric, it's all right. It's all right.'

But it wasn't.

I was full of such a hopeless fury, such unbelievable frustration at my uselessness, that I found to my horror that I was crying. I hadn't cried for years, but now I couldn't stop. Not discreet little snivels either, but great, tearing sobs, the kind that are so violent and huge they hurt your chest, till you feel you might split in half. I'd achieved nothing. I thought I had, but I hadn't been able to change a single thing. In the end, it all happens without you. Nothing you do or say or think or feel makes the slightest difference to anything. I'd come to help, but I'd only made it worse. And I loved Merwenna and I'd betrayed Leofric, but it was the two of them I could feel on either side of me now, holding me up.

I felt like shit.

And on top of it all, my head was full of the horrible pictures of the blood and slaughter of three-quarters of an hour ago. The sickening fear and violence. It all came crowding in on me, and I couldn't stop crying.

Merwenna pressed her free hand into the middle of my back.

'It's all right,' she said again. 'It will be all right, Joss. It will.'

CHAPTER FIFTEEN

※

ban hus
bone house (literal translation)

RIBCAGE

※

I var made Edmund kneel in front of him. He did this by having two of his heavies kick the legs away from under him, and then he offered him the kind of power-sharing deal that only an idiot would ever accept: ruling East Anglia as a puppet, making sure Ivar's rules were kept and Ivar's dues paid to him.

We heard him offer to spare Edmund's life if he renounced God and Christianity. It was insane. What the fuck did it matter what you believed in? And then I realised, it was just the excuse they gave themselves. The truth was, you were in this tribe or you were in that one, but the stronger tribe would beat the weaker one, and there would always be an excuse like a different religion or skin colour or 'this was my land first'. But in the end, it came down to who was the strongest. And it would carry on like that for another thousand years of history after today. It would still be like that when Rufus Palmier-Thompson took that David's poem off him and threatened to read it to the whole Year 11 common room. Because he was stronger, and he could.

Edmund didn't say anything in answer to this offer. He smiled instead, smiled and shook his head.

Watching while they dragged him away to the copse on the hill behind Haegelisdun was terrible. I knew exactly what was going to happen. The curved, cruel bows hooked onto the shoulders of the men who were hustling away were obscene, but I couldn't look away.

'You're shaking,' Merwenna whispered.

'Only the cold,' I lied.

She slipped her hand into mine. On the other side, I could see she was holding Leofric's hand as well.

'I saw you, under the bridge. Your helmet, in the sun, it reflected in the water,' Leofric said.

'I know you saw me.'

Eadwig's helmet, the one Cyneburga had polished so hard for me that it shone like gold. Not golden armour, just the sun on polished metal. And the marriage bit: Ivar had picked on Merwenna as the best way to get information out of Leofric because he'd seen his arm around her and guessed they were a couple. Even if he didn't know they were married. So over the next thousand years, the legend mutated into what we have now, the legend of Goldbrook:

the couple on their way to get married, the shining golden armour leading to the discovery of the king. You can easily see how it came about.

We waited like that, all of us pressed together for warmth. I didn't know how many hours were passing. I held onto Merwenna's hand like it was a lifebelt, and managed to get my sobs under control. The smoke smell had faded a bit, so I guessed everything the Vikings had torched had burnt down to ashes by now. We couldn't go back into the village because there were soldiers guarding us, so we just waited. We waited till Ivar and his men came back down the hill from the copse, laughing and looking pleased with themselves.

Ivar came up close to where we waited.

'Well, your king is in the wood. In little bits,' he said. The Danish soldiers with him laughed some more, and some of the people in the huddle of East Anglians started to wail and cry.

The wailing and the laughter scratched on my nerves. My teeth gritted themselves together, and my muscles tightened all over.

Someone came up to Ivar, and they embraced. The soldiers cheered.

'His name's Ubba,' Merwenna whispered to me under the noise of the cheers, 'he's the brother of Ivar the Boneless. Now they've joined forces, they're unstoppable. Nobody will be able to stand up to them.'

I turned my head to watch the two of them properly. Ivar and Ubba, the unstoppable force. Like a tank, crushing everyone in their path. But they were only men, just people like everybody else. We didn't have to be scared. I thought of Tracy, crushed by the tank of all those meetings over all those years, all those awful men. And Ms Osborne, and the 'I knew this would happen' in her eyes. I thought of Edmund, hacked into pieces in the wood. And Merwenna and Leofric and Penda and Cyneburga and Osthryd – decent people and friends of mine whose lives were as ruined as the burnt and ashy shells of the houses they used to live in.

Suddenly, I was angry. I was so angry I didn't care any more what they did to me. I just wanted to do what was right. And I'd had enough of being pushed around.

It felt like the whole of my life, and the whole of Tracy's before me, had been leading up to this moment.

'Merwenna,' I said.

'What is it, Joss?'

Her steady, greenish eyes looked into mine. The pattern the freckles made over the top of her nose was achingly familiar.

I pressed her hand to my mouth. I wanted to pull her to me for one last, glorious Hollywood kiss. But this wasn't the moment. This was real.

I had to show them. I had to show them you could stand up to Ivar and Ubba and all the rest of them, and even if it cost me my life – oh, God, even if it cost them *their* lives, it was worth doing. There were, I realised for the first time, worse things than dying.

'Watch. Watch,' I said.

I let go of Merwenna's hand.

And pushed my way out of the crowd. Slowly, slowly, because I knew that a frantic dash would mean a Viking axe in the face from one of the bodyguards that surrounded Ivar and Ubba. I kept my movements slow and my face calm and still.

Do the unexpected. They can't plan for that.

Possibilities flashed through my head.

I could spit in his eyes.

I could swear at him in fluent modern English.

I could shout out something punchy: 'No surrender!' or 'Freedom!'

But as I looked at Ivar the Boneless, at his cruel, complacent expression, consciousness of his victory written in every line of his face, something clicked inside me and I knew exactly what to do. I didn't need modern weapons and gadgets to frighten them. Julian was right; that would be playing them at their own game and what I needed was something different. Something they wouldn't expect.

I needed to make him see that although he had won the battle, that wasn't all there was. That the important bit of a person – the heart or soul or whatever you wanted to call it – couldn't be destroyed by violence or superior force or fear.

I held out my hands, palms uppermost, to show Ivar I wasn't armed.

'I want to talk to you. I want to tell you something,' I said. I said it loudly enough so Leofric and Merwenna and all the others could hear me.

Ivar laughed.

'Tell me something? What could you possibly have to say that I'd be interested in? I'm your conqueror. I've stamped on you and your race like a nest of cockroaches.'

I made sure I didn't drop my eyes.

Keep breathing.

'But I want to tell you something. It's important. I want to tell you I'm not afraid of you.'

He blinked. 'Well. Perhaps you ought to be. Look behind you at what we've done to your village. We've done the same thing to villages all over East Anglia. All over England. Go into the wood and see what we've done to your king. If you can find the bits.'

I kept my voice deliberately cool. I could see I was getting to him.

'Yeah, I know. But I'm still not afraid of you.'

One of the heavies took a step forward, but Ivar waved him back irritably. We were chest to chest now, like in a playground.

'Not afraid of me?'

'No,' I said.

'Listen, young hero,' he said. 'We have a torture for our enemies. It's called the Red Eagle. We open up your back, rib by rib, and take out your heart while it's still beating. We burn it in front of your eyes. It takes hours and hours to die. Still not afraid?'

I glanced behind me, at Leofric and Merwenna and what was left of Edmund's army. At what was left of Haegelisdun.

I knew I had to carry on, for them to understand that even though they'd lost, they hadn't lost everything. That fighting for what is right – freedom – even if you lose, is a kind of victory.

'Yeah, sounds very nasty. But I'm still not frightened.' I turned so I could see Merwenna and Leofric.

'I am not afraid of you!' I shouted.

Violence, whether it was the kind that killed people and burnt their homes to the ground, or the sort that happens in school playgrounds and toilets, isn't anything special. Being bigger or stronger than someone else is just that: bigger or stronger. Big deal. This was as true here, in this sad, smouldering, broken village in 869, as it had been in the boys' toilets at Easterbrook school. But although I knew that violence isn't the answer, I also knew you don't get peace by refusing to fight. It wasn't the answer, but sometimes it had to be part of the answer.

He was taller than I was. I had to stretch right up to bring the bony bit of my forehead crashing down onto the bridge of his nose. I heard, rather than felt, the eggshell splintering of cartilage, heard his yelp of pain and felt the warm spatter of blood against my own eyelids.

He staggered backwards, his hands up to his face. A surge of the purest joy ripped through me. I turned back to Merwenna with both my hands in the air like I'd just scored the winning goal at Wembley, and then it was all a blur: Ubba's furious face, a roar from the soldier behind me, Ubba's heavy axe smashing through the air; Merwenna's voice calling 'Joss' and then an explosion of light and sound like a starburst in my head as, I suppose, the axe hit me and after that, nothing.

Nothing. I opened my eyes to a pinkish world, feeling sleepy and warm and comfortable, and gradually realised I was lying in bed in the spare room at Cressida and Tim's house. The pink was from the sunlight filtering through the drawn curtains, and the windows were open because I could hear birds, and the curtains were fluttering in that dainty, feminine way they have when a light breeze is blowing. I couldn't see a clock, but it felt like the afternoon. Merwenna, Leofric, Penda, Aesc. They had all melted away in the teeth of the fiercest headache I had ever had. Even Edmund. I could remember them, of course I could, but I couldn't see any of them clearly any more. As if my head was full of fog.

'It's only concussion,' Cressida said when she came in to see if I was all right.

'Concussion?'

'Concussion,' she said firmly, settling my pillows for me like a nurse. 'Nothing that happened was your fault, Joss. It was because of the concussion.'

I shrugged; if she said so. I felt warm and lazy and as if what was going to happen next could go ahead and happen. I was happy just to be in bed and watch.

And in the days that passed, I became very grateful to that concussion: the police and the owner of the pharmacy had agreed not to press any charges because of it. They'd crumbled, faced with the medical expert Cressida had dredged up from somewhere, who said firmly that I'd been suffering from the effects of my first bang on the head, from falling down the quarry, at the time of the break-in. It hadn't been my fault. It had been a relief; not that I was afraid of the police and the courts and all that stuff, but it was so much better to be left alone.

Apart from the headache, I felt fine. But Cressida and Tim looked after me as tenderly as if was recovering slowly from a long illness, and I lay back against the pillows and let them. Julian came to see me every day, and drove me to the Norfolk and Norwich when I had to go for a scan to check if my brain was still functioning. And just as before, they found nothing wrong, apart from cuts and bruises and scratches from the battle with the Vikings and which they said must have happened when I fell into the church renovations.

'You must have had a blackout,' Julian said, 'climbing through the vestry window. You fell right into the builders' stuff, where they're repointing the west wall. Don't you remember anything about being outside the church?'

'Nothing,' I lied. I wondered whether to tell him where I'd been and what had happened, but in the end I didn't. I didn't want to fuck up again, not now everyone was being so nice to me and had decided that none of this was my fault.

The Hoxne GP came to see me and said I was on the mend but that I was to 'avoid excitement'. But I had visitors, which was quite exciting.

Tracy: Sofia brought her and Virginia and Sylvia to see me, and even relaxed her usual Serious expression into the smile suitable for a touching family reunion.

Alice: she texted 'how are you? xx' and the xx gave me hope. A day later, she came to see me, bringing a little bunch of yellow flowers that Cressida said were freesias. She was a bit shy and cool with me, which I suppose I was expecting. I didn't say I was sorry, about the lunch and everything, but I was, and I thought she knew that. I hoped so, anyway.

And David, the lovesick poet I'd saved from the school bullies, looking young and astonishing out of uniform and without his briefcase. We had nothing at all to say to each other, but I was glad he came.

And one other visitor.

Cressida knocked softly, then put her head around my door.

'There's a man to see you,' she said. 'He says he's your teacher. He's brought you some grapes and a Tupperware box full of rubbish.'

Poor Mr Richards. I didn't think he had anyone else to show his latest metal-detector finds apart from me, or maybe Julian.

'No more coins,' he said, 'but here are a couple of nails. Iron Age, I think. And this might be part of a brooch. And what do you think this is?'

I touched the object he gave me through its layers of polythene. It was the size of a clenched fist, swollen and lumpy with the centuries of decay under the mud. Exposed to the air, it was already crumbling into rusty orange flecks.

I knew exactly what it was.

'It's a comb,' I said. 'It's Leofric's second-best bone-handled comb. I must have dropped it by the river.'

Mr Richards patted my hand.

'I thought you'd recognise it,' he said. 'You know, I think you're much more of an expert about Anglo-Saxon history than you let on to me.'

I looked up at him sharply, and he smiled back, a nice smile – not like he was meaning anything by it or expecting me to say anything. I sighed.

'Are you all right, Joss?' he asked.

'Yeah. I'm all right,' I said, looking back at the comb. The idea of all the time that had passed since I last saw it was so enormous it was hard to think about.

He leant forward from where he was sitting, next to the bed.

'Hold out your hand flat,' he said, 'like you were going to feed a horse, that's right! I shouldn't really, but I don't think it matters too much. I mean, I don't think the British Museum are going to want it.'

I held out my hand like he said. I don't usually do exactly what I'm told, but you could trust Mr Richards.

Leofric's comb rolled out of its polythene wrapping onto my palm. The bone handle had gone, eaten away by the centuries, but there it was, real and true and undeniable in my hand.

'It's real,' I said, feeling its weight, 'it's actually real. It's as real as I am.'

When Mr Richards smiled, his face did that wrinkling-up thing again, like an old crisp packet.

'Of course it's real,' he said. 'History's as real as the two of us sitting here. Just a different time, that's all.'

'Yeah, I know,' I said. I did know, in theory, I mean. But the thing is, I wasn't good at believing in things that aren't there, things you can't see or hear or feel. Cressida and Tim could do it, but I wasn't that trusting. I saw now that some things can't necessarily be explained, but that didn't mean they weren't true.

Mr Richards cleared his throat.

'What are you planning to do, you know, after the summer holidays?...'

Surprising myself, I said 'I'm going back to Ipswich, if they let me. Take my A levels there.'

He made an agreeing sound.

'I mucked about for GCSEs. But I think I've probably scraped passes in them all,' I said.

He cleared his throat. 'But going back to Ipswich, doesn't that depend on...'

'The people at social services, yeah. What they decide to do about Tracy. She's a bit useless so they might decide to take us off her permanently. My sisters'll be adopted if that happens, because they're only two and people want babies. And me...I'll be in care permanently, I should think.'

My left hand was lying on the bed. Mr Richards took it and squeezed it, and his fingers were hard and bony.

See, normally I would hate this. But just like with

Cressida and her absent-minded pats, her 'it's all right Joss', somehow I didn't mind. There was just something about people like them.

'No point meeting trouble halfway, Joss,' he said, 'and I've got a feeling things are going to work out for you anyway.'

He stood up and started packing up his Tupperware box of treasures.

'A levels. You're going to have to start taking your education a whole lot more seriously,' he said.

'I'm going to,' I said.

I meant it. Up till then, I'd had no idea about taking education seriously, but now it was suddenly and inexplicably different. It was like someone had handed me a map of where to go from here, with a clear and obvious route to follow. I'd thought there was no point in working for anything – I'd thought I'd end up at exactly the same dead end as Tracy had. Because before the drinking and all the rest of it, she'd been clever, at least as clever as I was, and look at her now.

But now I felt different. In some weird way, the experience of Haegelisdun in 869 and Merwenna and Leofric and the death of Edmund had freed me to do exactly what I wanted with my life. My one precious life. When I was up and about again, I shyly tried to tell Mr Richards something of what I was feeling, and he seemed to know exactly what I meant and quoted some poetry at me about being the master of my fate and the captain of my soul.

Which is exactly what it felt like.

I considered different careers, like a woman trying on different dresses in a shop. The army? Medicine? Journalism? Something about the idea of writing for the papers appealed to me, but then I remembered from years ago the woman lawyer who'd come to see Tracy the first time the people at Social Care had wanted to put the twins (and me too, I suppose) on the Child Protection Register.

I thought to myself, 'I'll be a lawyer. I'll go to university, and I'll be a lawyer', testing the unfamiliar and suddenly exciting words. And then it was time to get out of bed and go back to Ipswich because Sofia and the rest of them decided that Tracy could have One Last Chance.

I hadn't expected it, not at all.

There was another meeting – like I said, they love them – and it was the same office with the walls the colour of phlegm, and the depressing view of the car park out of the windows. But there was something that was different this time. I didn't feel this time like nothing I said or Tracy said would make any difference. When Tracy said she'd decided to kick drinking (translated into Sofia-speak as Working Towards Becoming Alcohol Free), the suits around the table seemed pleased and offered her a place on a Women and Alcohol course. Which she accepted, as well as a place on another one, for Building her Self-Esteem.

Tracy was going to be so busy going on courses, there wouldn't be time for drinking binges, or accidentally setting the furniture alight.

And Sofia read out a statement from Cressida and Tim

in which they said how impressed they had been with my maturity and understanding, and with the positive relationships I'd built with teachers and local community leaders.

'Tracy can't do it on her own, Joss,' Sofia said. 'You need to know that you're a very important part of this plan. And we need to know that we can rely on you. If we can't, it's hard to see how you can remain together as a family. But if we can...'

'Of course you can rely on me. Of *course*,' I said.

I felt quite desperate for them to believe me.

'Look, things will be different from now on. I know how...how easy that sounds to say. I...oh, God, I just wish there was some way I could convince you.'

My voice came out far louder than I'd meant it to. I was terrified in case they didn't believe me. If only there was some sort of truth machine I could plug myself into, something that would remove doubt once and for all. Look, all those red lights mean it's true.

'We believe you, Joss,' Sofia said.

When she said this, I felt faint with relief. I sagged in my chair as though my bones had suddenly gone soft. My mouth muttered, 'thank you'.

'There will have to be regular safeguarding meetings and checks. Announced and unannounced visits. I will be in your life for quite a while, Tracy!'

Sofia smiled, as if this was a joke.

'But I think you can make this work. It's one last chance for you all.'

One last chance. I don't expect Tracy to turn into Mother of the Year, but you never know. And anyway, why should she? I'm helping her a lot more now; the other day I hoovered the whole of the new little flat they've found for us, and I'm always hanging the washing out. Sometimes making the tea, which I quite like doing. And Tracy is what she is, and that's all there is to it. She's my mum, and I'm her son. It'll have to do. She has remained Alcohol Free, and her self-esteem seems OK. And in September, term started again and I went back to the dump-school and worked with a new purpose.

My memories of Merwenna were so tender they were painful, like a sprained ankle or wrist. But as the weeks passed, it became a pain I quite liked. And I'll always have the scars.

When they said I could go home, I'd written a letter to Alice saying goodbye, and could we keep in touch? Cressida had promised to deliver it. I found I had forgiven Alice for her perfect skin and white sofas and house full of books and dentist father – he actually was a dentist, I found out later. For all the things, in fact, that she couldn't help.

I feel bad now about how I treated her. I hardly recognise the furious, bitter person I was then. She kept me waiting for a while, and who can blame her? But eventually she messaged me and now we see each other a bit. Quite a lot, actually, considering that now I'm back home, Hoxne – Hox-un – really does feel like the arse end of nowhere.

Alice and me. I don't know what will happen to the two of us. But I love her, I know that. I believe it. She had been kind to me when I'd been in trouble, and I'd been vile back. I'd seen the perfect skin and all the rest of it, and assumed that was all there was to her. I can't believe now I was that stupid, but like I said, I hardly recognise the person I was when I first came to Hoxne. Alice and me, it might end in tears, but some things are worth taking a risk for. And just because it might end in tears one day isn't enough of a reason to call it quits at the start. That's like saying, 'I don't want to live because one day I'll die.' You're finished before you even start, if you think like that. Sometimes, you have to trust. You have to believe in stuff, don't you? You have to believe in things or there's nothing left.